"Call me traditional if you like, as you said you were, but I believe marriage is not meant to be temporary, no matter if it is a love match or an arrangement."

He looked intensely at her and then continued. "Vows will be spoken. To me they will be sacred. If you accept me, I offer you all that I have or will have. As far as providing Scarsfeld with an heir, I will not force that upon you. The choice in the degree of intimacy in our marriage will be yours to make."

Her hair and her face must have all looked like one great flaming mess.

"You know that I cannot promise undying love. We have only just met." He took her hand, squeezed her glove. Even through the fabric she felt the heat where they joined. "What I can and do promise is my undying gratitude."

Honesty from him was quite a bit more than she had hoped for. Until this afternoon her only hope had been that he would be a bearable man to spend time with.

Isaiah Maxwell, while seeming severe, was honest. Forthright in what he wanted and what he had to offer. In spite of his apparent inability to present a genuine smile, she thought she liked him more than she didn't. And she did genuinely like his sister and care for her plight.

Author Note

This is a poem written by my eleven-year-old granddaughter, Brielle Iaccino, in response to something we would never have dreamed possible...social distancing. She wrote this one night before bedtime and I would like to share it with you because..."out of the mouths of babes"...

"In a day or two"

In a day or two we will cheer
A trembling world will be calm
We will reunite
The gates will open
We will sing with joy
I'll give you a hug
You'll give it back
We will be happy
And we shall hold hands
And Laugh
And Play
In a day or two
I will see you.

Coming to the end of a very trying and unusual year, I suspect that we all need a bit of Christmas cheer. I hope Felicia and Isaiah's story brings you a smile. I wish you all the hope, the joy and the love the season can bring.

"In a day or two we will cheer."

Wishing you the very best,
Carol and Brielle

CAROL ARENS

The Viscount's Yuletide Bride

HARLEQUIN®
HISTORICAL™

ISBN-13: 978-1-335-50585-9

The Viscount's Yuletide Bride

Copyright © 2020 by Carol Arens

Recycling programs
for this product may
not exist in your area.

This edition published by arrangement with Harlequin Books S.A.

For questions and comments about the quality of this book, please contact us at CustomerService@Harlequin.com.

Harlequin Enterprises ULC
22 Adelaide St. West, 40th Floor
Toronto, Ontario M5H 4E3, Canada
www.Harlequin.com

Printed in U.S.A.

Carol Arens delights in tossing fictional characters into hot water, watching them steam and then giving them a happily-ever-after. When she is not writing, she enjoys spending time with her family, beach camping or lounging about a mountain cabin. At home, she enjoys playing with her grandchildren and gardening. During rare spare moments, you will find her snuggled up with a good book. Carol enjoys hearing from readers at carolarens@yahoo.com or on Facebook.

Books by Carol Arens

Harlequin Historical

Dreaming of a Western Christmas
"Snowbound with the Cowboy"
Western Christmas Proposals
"The Sheriff's Christmas Proposal"
The Cowboy's Cinderella
Western Christmas Brides
"A Kiss from the Cowboy"
The Rancher's Inconvenient Bride
A Ranch to Call Home
A Texas Christmas Reunion
The Earl's American Heiress
Rescued by the Viscount's Ring
The Making of Baron Haversmere
The Viscount's Yuletide Bride

Visit the Author Profile page
at Harlequin.com for more titles.

To Brandon Matthew Iaccino.

My smart, thoughtful and generous grandson.
You are awesome and I love you.

Chapter One

Scarsfeld Manor—November 15, 1889

The letter in Isaiah Elphalet Maxwell's hand stung like a ball of ice—or perhaps it burned as if he crushed a live flame.

He stared out of the conservatory windows watching his young half-sister play on the shore of Lake Windermere, his heart feeling as if it were being crushed between his boot heel and a stone.

Abigail leapt, twirled in the air, then presented a deep curtsy to her cat, Eloise.

How could he not smile at her antics? Even with the letter crushed in his trembling fist, how could he not?

Eight-year-old Lady Abigail Elizabeth Turner was the one bright spot in his rather bleak home. In his life, really.

She was his, by blood and by right.

Ever since that rainy night eight years ago when his butler carried a dripping, screeching bundle into the parlour followed by a harried-looking fellow who turned out to be his late stepfather's lawyer, Isaiah's life had not been the same.

Half-brother—yes, he was that to Abigail—but father, too. He was the one to have cared for her, loved and nurtured her all her life. In spite of the fact that he had been only twenty-two at the time, no natural father could have been more devoted.

Spinning about, he stalked towards the fireplace, flung the missive into the flames, then returned to the window.

The wind was rising, dancing through the tree tops and scattering the last of the autumn leaves across the ground.

Naturally, Abigail did not appear to mind the cool bluster in the least. She chased the brightly hued foliage about, stomping and laughing. Her tortoiseshell cat frolicked about her skirt, swatting the lace hem.

It was time to call her inside. While it was not likely that a weakened branch would crack, fall and strike her, it could not be discounted out of hand.

Experience had taught him that he could not be too watchful when it came to keeping a child safe. An unlocked door on a freezing night had taught him that lesson.

Besides, even from here he could see the nanny shivering in her coat while stomping her feet as if that might somehow warm her.

Coming out on to the terrace, he stood for a moment bearing the cold in order to gaze at the lake. Wide and long, it resembled a frigid blue ribbon cutting the land.

Isaiah looked down the gentle slope leading to the

shore. He waved his arm to get his sister's attention. Wind caught the lapels of his coat and flapped them about.

Truly, he disliked this time of year. Hopefully it would not snow any time soon. The further they went into autumn and winter without it, the better it would be for everyone.

Seeing his signal to come inside, Abigail scooped up her cat and dashed up the stone steps. Out of breath, she wrapped her slender arms about his ribs and pressed her ear against his heart.

'Will it snow, Isaiah?' She hopped up and down, which made the cat wriggle out of her arms and leap inside the open door of the conservatory.

Well, lack of snow would be better for most people, but clearly not his little sister.

The nanny, her shoulders hunched, hurried past, following the cat.

'If it does, at least we will remain properly inside the manor as sensible people should,' she muttered in passing.

It did not seem to matter that he was Viscount Scarsfeld—the ninth one, in fact—nor that his social position outranked hers. Miss Shirls spoke her mind.

On that night when Abigail had arrived the woman had been summoned from her duties in the kitchen. With a bottle of warm milk in hand, she took the screeching baby. Before the bottle was fully suckled, Miss Shirls appointed herself nursemaid. He had allowed it since he'd had no one else. As it turned out, the transition from kitchen to nursery had worked well for Miss Shirls and for him.

Miss Shirls had been devoted to his sister every day since. He supposed it was fair and just to overlook her familiarity. Status notwithstanding, the nanny did feel as though she was family.

As family went it was only he and Abigail. If Miss Shirls placed herself with them, he did not mind in the least.

'I want to play outdoors in the snow! I shall build half a dozen snowmen and snow cats. Will you help me, Isaiah?'

He kissed the top of her head where her hat had fallen off. Her blonde curls smelled like cold, fresh air. Could one actually smell happiness? If so, he smelled that on her, too.

Making sure Abigail grew up happy was what mattered most to Isaiah. He would do whatever was needed to keep her from the loneliness he had suffered in childhood.

As long as he drew a breath she would know every day that she was cherished.

No matter that he had tossed the letter from his late stepfather's brother into the flames, the words remained seared on his fingers, burned into his brain.

He read them over in his mind. He did not wish to, but could not seem to help it, no matter how he tried.

Greetings, Lord Scarsfeld,
My wife and I hope all is well with you as we approach Christmas time—a holiday we have been negligent in celebrating with you and our dear niece Abigail.'

Their 'dear niece Abigail' whom they had never set eyes upon.

We will, however, make amends for it this year. We do appreciate that you have taken on the burden of raising her. We are forever grateful.

As if they had just due to be grateful for anything.

But now the time has come for my wife and I to lift that burden.

Abigail had never been, nor would she ever be, a burden to be lifted.

It seems only right and appropriate, since you remain unmarried and my lovely Diana has yet to bless us with a child of our own, that our niece should be raised at Penfield. I trust this is agreeable.
Please look forward to our arrival on the fifteenth of December.
With kind regards,
Penfield

Why would Penfield decide this now? In all of Abigail's eight years they had not visited or asked for her to visit them. A rare letter was all she had received from the Earl and Countess of Penfield.

The best he could make of it was that they had given up hope of having a child of their own and had now set their sights upon his sister. Perhaps they thought

London could offer advantages that a quiet life here could not.

'You look like thunder, Isaiah.' Abigail slashed her slim brows at him in censure. 'It is no wonder people think you are forbidding.'

'Who thinks it?'

'Nearly everyone. You ought to smile upon occasion so they do not think you so imperious.'

'Imperious?'

'Or crusty.'

'Crusty!' He was only thirty years old and years away from being crusty!

'Do you think I'm crusty?' Please let her not.

'I know you are not. You can be great fun when you want to be and you have the kindest soul of anyone. Although you do your best to hide it.'

'Why would I?'

'It is the very question I ask.'

'You seem older than eight years.'

'And you seem grumpier than you are.'

He did have a reputation for being glum—even surly—he had heard some whisper that sentiment. People did not seek his company unless it was necessary. Which was fine since he preferred to avoid what was to him the false merriment of social gatherings, where at every turn young ladies and their mothers vied for his attention—for his title, more to the point.

On the occasions where he had to attend a function, presenting the darker side of his nature had given him a buffer of sorts.

His distant behaviour did keep him isolated from

society for the most part, but it did not overly trouble him. He was rather satisfied with the way things were. Quiet, orderly, predictable—it was how he liked his life.

'What would you do if you were me? To make people think I'm not crusty?'

'Smile more, of course. Perhaps laugh out loud. And put a Christmas tree in the parlour.'

A Christmas tree! He had not put up one of those since he was a child—and, no, even for Abigail he could not do it.

'I never knew you wanted one.'

'Everyone does, you know. Ribbons on the stairway and bows on the mantel can only bring so much Christmas cheer. As much as I enjoy the Yule log, I'm eight years old now and it is past time I had a tree.'

'This is the first time you've brought up the subject.'

'And it will not be the last. I've seen them in town, how lovely they are. In all the books people sing carols while gathered about them…and while eating sugar plums! What must Father Christmas think? Asking him to come into a home with no tree is rather disrespectful.'

Perhaps he ought to try to set aside his bitter resentment of Christmas trees. It was probably unreasonable to tie his crushed childhood to them. It was not a tree's fault that his stepfather had been a beast, or that his mother had chosen him and cast off her small son.

He ought to be reasonable about it—yet he found he could not. He would give his sister anything—anything but that symbol of his deepest grief.

'Would you rather live somewhere else, Abigail? Somewhere that can offer you more?' Of course she was far too young to make such a choice, but given the letter from her uncle, he did need to know.

He clasped her small hand and led her into the conservatory. She clung tight to him and remained oddly silent.

Once inside he unbuttoned her coat and slid it off her.

'Are you sending me away?' she asked, her voice small and quavering.

'No! Never—why would you think it?'

'Some girls are sent away. They have to go to boarding school and learn to be proper ladies. Is it why you have not yet hired a governess to teach me?'

'Abigail, I would never send you anywhere you do not wish to go. I promise I will not.' Her relieved smile showed off the gap of a missing tooth. Her customary blue-eyed sparkle returned.

Isaiah's throat tightened when the ghost of their mother skittered across her face. Their mother when she was young, before she married Palmer Turner, Fifth Earl of Penfield.

'But it is true that you are growing up quicker than your cat can dash after a mouse. I can see you getting taller by the hour. You will need someone to teach you to be a lady. There is more to it than one would guess.'

'Someone who will live here with us?' Once again she looked suspiciously at him. 'A governess, or a tutor?'

'I was thinking more of a female relative.'

'Lady Penfield is the only one. I believe she will not leave Penfield.'

'I must marry. It is past time that I did.' His sister's

mouth popped into a perfectly surprised circle. 'How would you feel about that?'

Having a wife could only go in his favour when Lord and Lady Penfield came. He must do whatever he could to dissuade the Earl and the Countess from taking Abigail. If the issue went to court, he would lose. A married earl would be given custody over a crusty unwed viscount by any judge.

'I'd feel a lot of things about it. But you know you must make an effort to smile at a wife or she will not be happy here.'

'What I want to know is if you will be happy.'

'It would be rather like having a mother in a sister. Yes, I would like that. But—will you love me less when you love her, too?'

'Nothing in this world could make me love you less. Besides, it is not required to love one's wife. There are happy marriages founded on friendship.'

'If you truly thought so, you would have married by now.'

Or if his mother had found a scrap of happiness in her second marriage, he might have a more hopeful outlook on the prospect.

'Honestly, Abigail, are you really only eight years old?'

'I'm an eight-year-old girl, which makes all the difference. Were I a boy, all I would want to do is climb things and run about making mischief. You have seen the stableman's son?'

'I am forever grateful to have a sister. But do I have your approval?'

'You do, just as long as the lady approves of cats.'

London—early December, 1889

It did not appear that it was going to snow while Felicia snipped branches. Given that the clouds dotting the sky were no more than wispy puffs, it was not likely to drizzle either.

To her mind it might as well be spring in the garden of Cliverton House, with birds singing and flowers budding.

It was enough to make a holly-gatherer weep.

Christmas was supposed to be crisp and lovely.

Pausing with the clipper blades poised over a branch, she did have to admit that it was crisp and lovely. At the same time she had to remind herself that it was not in the spirit of the season to be imagining spring.

At least her fingers were chilled, her nose red with the lovely nip in the air. There was even a cup of hot cocoa close at hand, spewing fragrant steam into the garden.

Perhaps it would not snow or rain, but she carried on snipping evergreen branches with a smile. After all, Christmas was coming regardless if it arrived white and frigid or green and mild.

All things considered the weather did not really matter. Christmas was the most wonderful time of the year no matter the circumstances.

Her sisters, Cornelia and Ginny, grumbled that it was far too early to celebrate it. Of course they were not the ones to be named Felicia Merry.

Names were important. It was Felicia's belief, and her late mother's as well, that names had meaning, they were not simply fetching titles. Mama had often pointed out that was the reason why no one named their sons Beelzebub or the daughters Jezebel.

Funny how thinking of her mother made her smile and weep all in one tender emotion.

Time and again, she had found Mama's name theory to be true.

In Felicia's case it certainly was. As her name suggested, she nearly always saw the bright side of things.

'Happy times.' Mama had been fond of telling her what her name meant, of how she and father had thought and prayed upon it before naming her.

'Happy times' also described Christmas and so she had no problem whatsoever beginning to celebrate this early.

Cornelia could be excused for having her mind on other things than Christmas. She had recently become engaged to a very suitable earl. No doubt Mother and Father were gazing down and feeling very proud of their eldest child.

Ginny might come outside to join her once she put down her journal and put on her spectacles.

Spectacles she did not really need for seeing clearly. Her younger sister, by one year only, was an irresistible beauty and Felicia knew she donned them in an attempt to keep the young swains at bay.

Indeed, with her sunny curls and eyes the lavender-blue shade of a harebell blossom, she was quite sought after.

A situation which did not please her sister at all. Poor Ginny was as shy and as timid as a newborn fawn.

With the solicitor meeting with Peter in the study at the moment, Ginny would not come down without wearing her big, black glasses. Like every other man, the fellow was smitten with her.

From above, Mother and Father were probably congratulating themselves on naming her Virginia to ensure that she did not fall headlong over every gentleman wanting to woo her with flattery.

At least Mother and Father need fear nothing of the kind where Felicia was concerned. She was neither pretty nor petite. She quite towered over her sisters. To her knowledge she had never turned a man's head. There were occasional suitors, but they were halfhearted wooers, being more interested in what Father's title had to offer them than in her. For most of them it took no more than half an hour of being looked down upon—or having to gaze up at her—to send them searching for a more fetching lady.

An overly tall, red-haired and green-eyed woman was no one's first choice.

After three Seasons with no offer of marriage, she was quite firmly on the shelf. In another year she would become positively dusty.

Which was not a horrid thing. No, not really.

Surely a woman could lead a satisfactory life without a husband to dictate how merry she could feel, especially at Christmas? Living at Cliverton House with her sisters and her cousin, Peter, who was now Cliverton in Father's stead, was a satisfactory existence.

She tried not to think of how this would all change once her sisters married and once her cousin took a wife—and, really, at thirty years old it was time he did. Everything was bound to change then. It was mortifying to see herself being dependent upon her cousin and his future wife's good will for every little thing.

'Lady Cliverton, I would like a new bonnet, if it is not too much trouble,' she mumbled, imaging she might one day say such a thing.

Still, for the moment she was the unattached cousin of Viscount Cliverton and she was, for the greater part, free to act as she pleased.

For instance, when she decided to decorate the parlour on the first day of December no one forbade it. While it was true that they considered her actions a wee bit eager, no one prevented her from draping holly over the fireplace mantel and red ribbons on the banister.

A husband might stay her hand, douse her joy. Not all men were enthusiastic about celebrating Christmas. She was better off unwed than being bound to a cheerless man.

Was she not?

As it was now, she was free to trim greenery with no grumpy fellow to cast a frown.

She could sing carols while she did it.

'"I saw three ships come sailing in, on Christmas Day, on Christmas Day. I saw three ships come sailing in on Christmas Day in the morning."'

It did feel glorious to sing. There were few things she loved more.

She went up on her toes to snip a branch that her sisters would not be able to reach. They would be forced to summon a gardener to do it. Even Peter would have to stretch on his toes to manage.

'"And what was in those ships all three, On Christmas Day on Christmas Day—"'

'Screeching cats.' Peter's voice, so unexpected, nearly made her drop the shears.

'Take this,' she said and handed him the branch she had just cut.

Her cousin often made jest of her singing voice. It was difficult to take offence since she knew he stated the obvious with affection.

Sadly, in spite of the fact that she adored singing, she could not carry a tune.

'You do realise that by Christmas Day these will be dried out?'

'In the event, I will simply cut more.'

Peter might be her cousin, but he felt more like a brother. After the death of Felicia's aunt and uncle, he had come to live at Cliverton House so they had been raised together.

Father had made no secret of the fact that he was delighted to have his heir presumptive under his roof. Felicia always felt that Mother and Father had loved their nephew with the same affection they bore their own children.

Love was the abiding spirit at Cliverton. Even more so with Christmas so close at hand. Why, already she imagined the house scented with evergreen branches.

'It is a nice morning, Felicia. Will you sit in the sun-shine with me for a moment?'

For all that he called this a nice morning, his expression appeared drawn.

'It is lovely, even though it is not my first choice for weather this time of year.'

Peter cleared his throat, tugged at his cravat while

she sat down beside him on the garden bench. He looked rather as though he was sitting on a drawing pin.

'Choice is a thing we do not always have, wouldn't you agree?'

Why was his mouth drawn tight? It did not appear that he was about to break into a smile at the pleasure of spending a few moments with her.

'Yes, of course,' she said. 'There are times when we must muddle through, regardless of circumstances.'

'I hope this is something you believe and not a mere platitude.'

'I'm beginning to feel that I hope I believe it, too.' She suspected this was not simply an idle conversation on a pleasant day.

A movement on the steps caught her attention— Ginny standing on the porch, wringing her hands in front of her and looking like spoiled milk.

Clearly Felicia needed to hurry with the Christmas decorating. Something was going to need muddling through. A bit of cheer would only help.

'Yes, well you might. Felicia, the solicitor has brought—news.'

'Are we to assume it is not good news?'

One only needed to look at Ginny, her glasses clenched in her fist, to know it was true.

'You had best tell me what the problem is before I imagine the worst.' As clearly Ginny had already done.

'Viscount Scarsfeld is requesting a bride.'

Chapter Two

Scarsfeld!

'Surely not!'

After all this time?

'I thought he had forgotten about us,' Cornelia declared.

Felicia's insides whirled in confusion.

'We all assumed he did not wish to marry.' Ginny hurried down the garden steps, her hand clutched in a fist over her heart.

Cornelia rushed out of the door, following close behind.

'He gave every indication of it when last we saw him at Lady Newton's ball,' her older sister stated, nodding as if she remembered the occasion of meeting him as though it had been last week.

The fact of it was, Lady Newton's ball had been three years ago when Felicia and Ginny were freshly come out.

'Perhaps he does not wish it. Men often wed even without wishing to,' Cornelia added to her thought.

'Peter, are you certain he is asking for one of us?'

'I'm sorry but, yes. The Viscount has sent along a letter which his solicitor says he discovered among his mother's belongings when she died eight years ago. It is a letter which both his mother and yours wrote together expressing their fondest wishes that "Sweet little Isaiah should one day wed one of the darling Penney-jons girls."'

'But he is not sweet!' Ginny's eyebrows slashed a frown over eyes creased in worry. 'Why, as I recall it, he did not smile at anyone at the ball, nor did he ask anyone to dance.'

'Perhaps he was simply out of sorts for some reason or another,' Felicia pointed out because it only seemed fair to do so.

'I would think you would be less charitable with regard to the man,' Cornelia said. 'You are the one he blanked, after all.'

'I hardly remember that.' Truly, she had been ignored by so many gentlemen over the last three years that she barely recalled the moment. And who could blame him for it? She had been a blushing debutante while he had been a mature, experienced man.

The only reason she had approached him was because she remembered how Mama always spoke so fondly of him and his mother.

Felicia had been too young to remember Mama's friend, but Mama had told many stories of them growing up together as close as sisters.

She did not need to read the letter as proof of how much Mama wished for one of her girls to wed Juliette Scarsfeld's son. Until Mama and Father passed away

ten years ago in a carriage accident, she had listened
to Mama tell of her cherished dreams.

Until this moment that was all they had ever been.

When Lord Scarsfeld had been pointed out to her
at the ball she had stared in awe at the man because of
Mama, imagining how pleased she would have been to
introduce her girls to him and to begin matchmaking.

Yes, his gaze had passed over her without even engaging her eye, but it had not really stung. The fact that
he also blanked Ginny made her feel oddly better about
the experience.

'The letter is not binding, you understand,' Peter
explained.

'Perhaps not, but we all know how Mama longed for
just this,' Cornelia said.

'Surely she would not expect us to go through with
it after all this time,' Ginny said, unable to cover the
hiccup in her voice.

Cornelia sighed, lifting her shoulders in apparent res-
ignation of what had befallen them. As well she might
since she was betrothed and safely unavailable. 'A marriage between our families would honour her memory
as nothing else would.'

It was true, yet it was a rather drastic way to do so.

'I am saddened to read that Mama's friend has passed
away.' Cornelia shook her head, the expression in her
bright blue eyes dimmed. 'I recall that she and her little
boy used to visit. But only until she remarried.'

'We need not wonder how her son turned out. We
saw his sullen nature for ourselves,' Ginny said with a
shudder she made no attempt to suppress.

'Which of my sisters has he asked for, Peter?' Cornelia tapped her fingers on the waist to her gown, looking more curious than alarmed. As well she might, being safely removed from the choosing.

A profound silence settled over the garden.

It was as if even the breeze held its breath waiting for the answer.

Oh, but surely it could not be Ginny! She was far too timid for a man like him—or, more accurately, the one they recalled him to be. Although, of course, shy and timid girls were required to marry as well as anyone else was.

But if on the odd chance he did remember them, it would be Ginny he chose. Any man would.

'Who has he chosen, Peter?' Felicia had to ask because the tense silence could not go on. It was as if an axe were poised over them and the sooner it fell, the sooner the situation could be muddled through.

Please do not let it be Ginny, she prayed silently. Her sister was not much of a muddler. She was as likely to plunge headlong into despair as anything else.

'Yes, well…apparently he has left the choice up to us…or you, rather.' Peter glanced between her and Ginny.

'We will take our time and make a decision,' Felicia announced, taking Ginny's hand and squeezing it. 'Nothing needs to be settled in the moment.'

For all that she wanted to jump in and martyr herself for her sister's sake, she could not quite gather her legs for the leap.

Peter stood up, walked a few steps along the garden path. When he spotted a small stone, he kicked it hard into a tree trunk.

'Unfortunately,' he muttered without looking up, 'there is no time. Lord Scarsfeld is requesting that one of you come to Windermere with all haste.'

When Peter did turn he was staring at Felicia, not Ginny.

Of course, everyone would assume she would be the one to fill the role. Even she understood this would be her one chance to get a husband given that Lord Scarsfeld was not particular about whom he wed. His only requirement was for her to be a Penneyjons.

Perhaps he wished to fulfil his mother's wishes as much as she wished to fulfil Mama's.

Oh, she could nearly feel her mother's giddiness from above. Although Mama had passed away before Felicia's Season began, she surely noticed, in whatever way the dearly departed had of noticing, that their middle daughter would not find a husband on her own.

Some might say she should be grateful for the chance to wed.

Spinsterhood was a humiliating state and one to be avoided at all costs.

Felicia would argue that, so far, it was not at all horrid.

But it would not be long before she would watch her sisters and her cousin wed. She would see them bringing babies into the family, watch their joy overflow the house, while she sat in a chair and knitted her nieces and nephews socks.

'Perhaps he is not so wretched,' Ginny said with a fragile smile, now that she was not the one likely to have to make the choice. 'I do recall Mother telling the story of how adorable little Isaiah was and how he used to lead you about by the hand when you were learning to walk—and how you laughed and laughed.'

'Yes!' Cornelia clapped her hands. 'I had nearly forgotten! Mama said you used crawl after him, wailing when he let go of your hand.'

Perhaps, but what had that to do with anything now? Felicia scarcely recalled what the man looked like three years ago, let alone any memory of crawling after him as a baby.

Those were Mama's cherished memories, not hers. Oh, but she did cherish her mother. Even now, after all this time and with the mysterious distance which separated the mortal and the immortal, she wanted to please her mother.

Yes, it would honour Mama to fulfil her dearest wish, but there was more to it. She would also honour her mother by watching out for Ginny. Felicia believed her sister would not thrive being married to a man like Viscount Scarsfeld.

Felicia stood up, yanked the folds of her skirt into order. 'Very well. I will travel north to meet him.'

'I will go along.' Ginny bravely lifted her chin, offering up her life to fate—and her sister. 'It is only right. Perhaps we did misunderstand him, or he might have changed.'

It was probably fair to allow the man to choose between Felicia and her sister.

Certainly it was, yet, given the choice, he would pick Ginny.

Which would leave Felicia free of obligation—and laden with guilt for ever.

'I feel that it would be unkind of you to risk my one

chance to have a husband, Ginny. You are pretty. You will have your choice of a dozen proposals to accept whenever you wish to.'

Peter opened his mouth, but Felicia shushed him by slashing a sidelong frown.

'Please give me my chance to meet Lord Scarsfeld. If he rejects me, then you may have a chance with him.'

Saying those words brought her up short. He might well reject her. He had overlooked her at Lady Newton's ball.

It was one thing to be passed over at a social gathering, quite another to be rejected as a bride.

The humiliation would be crushing.

'He will not turn you away, Felicia,' Peter said softly as if reading her mind. 'I'm given to understand that he requires a wife in all haste. If you agree to this, you will become Lady Scarsfeld within a fortnight.'

Muddle through, muddle through, she repeated the mantra in her mind a dozen times while stating out loud, 'How lovely. What a grand adventure it will be.'

The lie was worthwhile if only to see Ginny's face take on a bit of colour.

And perhaps the words held an ounce of truth. One's attitude towards a situation often made it a blessing or a curse.

How many times had she stood beside Cornelia while they watched a glowering sky? Her sister would grumble about the horrid weather coming while Felicia looked at up in anticipation of rain tapping merrily on her umbrella?

She would muddle through this and do her best to keep a smile about it.

* * *

Standing in the centre of the parlour, Isaiah turned in a circle, judging the room with a critical eye. How would a stranger view it? The stranger he was going to wed, in fact?

It was a welcoming space for all its size, in his estimation. Wood-panelled walls gleamed with polish. A large rug in shades of red and gold warmed the floor in front of a fireplace so huge that the flames cast the entire room in a cosy glow.

The banisters of the wide staircase which he had played upon as a child rose to a landing where a trio of stained-glass windows cast reflections of red, blue and green on the floor.

Even now he could see a crack in one of panes. When he was four years old he had thought it would be a fine thing to toss a ball at the window in the hopes of it breaking a hole in it large enough for a bird to fly inside.

Mother had laughed, ruffled his hair and assured him all was well. A week later she purchased a pair of budgerigars. She never did repair the window, claiming it gave the house character.

He shook his head, nipping the inside of his lip. It was better not to think of those times. In the end the sweet memories turned bitter.

Left to his own inclinations the house would be a grey, sombre place. It was for Abigail's sake he kept the fireplaces cheerfully snapping, colourful paintings on the walls and flowers or whatever greenery was to be found this time of year in vases all over the mansion.

He would do anything to make sure his sister knew she was loved and appreciated.

Which included marrying a stranger if that was what it took to keep her with him.

It had been ten days since he had had word from Lord Cliverton that his daughter would fulfil the wish of their mothers and wed him.

Circumstances prevented all the typical celebrations involved in arranging a wedding.

Would Miss Penneyjons mind it so much? It was not as if they were celebrating their love—or even their friendship.

The one and only thing he felt for her was gratitude. He could not appreciate her beauty since he had no idea what she looked like. Nor could he admire her wit. For all he knew she was dull—or she might be bright and charming. The only knowledge he had of her was a vague memory of holding a tiny hand, of a screeching baby crawling madly after him—and that her name was Felicia, which he would not have recalled on his own, but the names of all the Penneyjons daughters were in the letter he had found among his mother's belongings.

The only thing that mattered in the end was that Miss Penneyjons had consented, although he was left wondering why. Was the woman as desperate to be wed as he was?

Whatever her motivation, he would welcome her. One of the reasons Lord Penfield had given for wanting custody of Abigail was that Isaiah was not married.

In a few days he would be. The Earl's argument in that area would be crushed.

If the reason they wanted Abigail had to do with them having no child of their own, there was nothing he could do about that.

But damn it all! His sister was happy living here. He would not have her ripped away from Scarsfeld as he had been.

Isaiah had no wish to marry, but clearly, if he had any hope of Abigail remaining with him, he must.

It would have been right to travel to London and offer Miss Penneyjons a proper proposal, but time would not allow for it.

Time was precisely what he needed more of. It was important for the Earl and the Countess to witness an easy rapport between Isaiah and his bride.

As it was, he feared she would barely have time to settle in, let alone portray an image of contentment.

Settle in, yes—but settled in where? Not the master's chamber, certainly. It was one thing to ask the woman to be his wife, but quite another to expect she would be willing to become his lover.

Perhaps in time—once they became acquainted and—

'You look more dour than usual, my lord,' Miss Shirls commented as she hurried past him with a stack of books she must be carrying to his sister's quarters. She paused to frown at him. 'No doubt it has to do with your hasty decision to take a stranger as a bride.'

Thankfully she said so under her breath. While Miss Shirls felt free to speak to him this way, she did not feel the rest of staff had the same privilege.

'As it happens, I am wondering what to do with her.'

'Surely not!' The nanny did not blush when she turned back with a wink.

'Where to put her.' Oddly enough, despite having a

reputation as the harshest man in Windermere and beyond, he blushed rather easily.

'If there is to be no heir, then I would suggest your
late mother's room.'

With a nod she was off to deliver the books to Abigail.

The Viscountess's chamber did make the most sense
since Miss Penneyjons would be Viscountess Scarsfeld
within a matter of days.

So be it, then. He mounted the steps towards the
third-storey rooms. It had been a very long time since
he had entered his late mother's chamber.

The staff saw to its care regularly, but they did not
suffer the attack of grief that was sure to overtake him
the instant he opened that door.

Not grief for her death, although he did grieve that,
but because it was where so much joy had lived—and
perished. There had been a time when his mother was
his whole world—a time when he had been hers.

He opened the door slowly. Nothing was the same as
it had been when he was seven years old. Everything
that had belonged to his mother had been replaced long
ago. He had no wish to keep his home a museum.

But still, she was there: standing in the doorway,
laughing while she gazed at him; then later weeping;
and in the end staring at him from the nursery doorway, blank and silent.

Worse than the weeping and the silence was the distance. On that last day, Christmas Eve, when she had
stood in his doorway just as he was now standing in
hers, there had been no emotion in her eyes. He might

have been a neighbour's child for all there was left between them.

Perhaps having a new Lady Scarsfeld residing in the chamber was for the best. It could hardly be worse, at least.

Of all the things he wondered about where Felicia Penneyjons was concerned, the most important was how she would get along with Abigail.

It was crucial that she did, he thought while closing the door and turning his back on the room and its ghosts. He hoped Lord and Lady Penfield would think twice about ripping apart a loving family.

The opposite was true as well. If Miss Penneyjons and Abigail did not suit, they could feel justified in taking her.

Standing alone in the hallway, he considered what Abigail had said about smiling—how he ought to do it more often.

All right, then. He lifted his cheeks, but wondered if his teeth ought to show or not. The gesture, offered for show, felt awkward.

Suddenly the door across the hallway opened. Miss Shirls stepped out of the room with a different load of books in her arms.

'Are you going to attack me, my lord?'

There was his answer. No teeth. A socially motivated smile must be presented with his lips closed.

Felicia's sisters asked to accompany her and Peter to Scarsfeld. She turned them down. They did not really want to go, but felt guilty for her having to face 'Sir Gloomy' alone.

That was what they had taken to calling Lord Scarsfeld: Sir Gloomy, or, at times, Lord Scowl.

It wasn't fair, of course. None of them had ever had a conversation with the man. He might have a perfectly lovely disposition for all they knew. They had only seen him, as an adult, that one time and perhaps there had been a reason for his moodiness.

Gazing out the train window, Felicia watched pastureland appear and then drift away with an occasional cow or sheep to return her gaze.

Shifting her gaze to Peter seated on the plush crimson bench across from her, she was so nervous it felt as though bees buzzed about inside her. When they were ten minutes away from Windermere Station, she had no fear that her cousin was suffering any anxiety.

His head nodded towards his chest while he blissfully snored.

If only she could feel such calm. Of course her cousin was going to go home next week to carry on with his life.

With a mental shake, she reminded herself that she was also going to carry on with her life. She did not know precisely what that life would be like, but she had no option but to carry on with it.

Not unless she wanted to let her family down and ignore her mother's wishes. Not unless she wanted Ginny to come in her stead.

And especially if she did not wish to become the pitiful Penneyjons spinster, cooing over everyone's children but her own.

There had been times when she thought she might manage life that way, but now that this new path had opened she wondered if she had been forcing herself to think it because she had no choice about it.

Looking for the bright side of things and all that.

Of course she could be doing the same thing now. Feeling she had no choice in the marriage, was she now looking for the best in it?

Perhaps she was one who just muddled through whatever life presented. She did have to wonder if muddling was a step short of being fulfilled.

At least Windermere was reported to be an exceptionally lovely village. Indeed, beyond the train window everything looked properly cold and grey for this time of year. The glass felt frigid when she pressed her fingers against it.

Peter had been all for going immediately to Scarsfeld as soon as they stepped off the train. Felicia wanted to spend a night in town before heading to the estate and she held firm to it. One did not toss a fish into new aquarium water and hope for it to survive. No, indeed, it needed a few hours to acclimatise.

She fully intended on taking a day to acclimatise, to tour Windermere, get used to the sights, sounds and people. After that she would proceed to the estate which was said to be only a few miles north of town.

A place where, she had heard, it was not uncommon for snow to cover the ground at Christmas.

While Peter continued to snore, Felicia wondered about Scarsfeld. What was it like? Cheerful? Glum? Had anyone begun to decorate for the swift approach of Christmas?

Perhaps not. If Lord Scarsfeld actually was a gloomy scowler, he might not think to do it.

A part of her hoped he had not. Decorating her new home would help her bond with it, make her feel as if she had a place and a purpose.

Yes! A purpose was exactly what she needed.

Lord Scarsfeld had not revealed why he needed to marry in such a hurry, but she assumed she played a rather large part in whatever it was. There was bound to be some sort of purpose involved in her role as Lady Scarsfeld.

Whatever it turned out to be it had to far outshine a spinster's purpose which was, to her mind, providing an object of pity, becoming an example for young ladies not to follow—that and knitting endless pairs of extra socks for nieces and nephews.

One by one her fellow passengers began to stretch and stand in anticipation of arriving at the station.

The whistle shrilled. Felicia reached across and jiggled Peter's shoulder. He blinked, glancing about fuzzy-eyed.

'Do you wonder,' she asked while rising and shrugging into her coat, 'if I might have been sent here for a reason?'

She buttoned up, then attached her hat to her hair. The weather did look rather foreboding.

'You know you have. To get married and honour your mother's wishes. And to make a life for yourself, Felicia.' Peter stood, peered out the window and fastened his coat. 'It looks like a beast of a day.'

'There is that, of course—for Mama. But it is what you said about starting a new life…' It was funny how she thrilled to the idea and at the same time recoiled from it. It was a distinctly unsettling feeling. 'There must be some sort of purpose for me in it that I am not yet aware of.'

'To make a bear purr? Knowing you, you might have it in mind to encourage Lord Scarsfeld to amend his sullen ways.'

'An unknown purpose can be a mysterious thing, so perhaps that is it. But we do not know for certain that the Viscount is sullen.'

'If he is and anyone can bring him round, it is you.'

Maybe. But if he was the man her sisters feared him to be it would be a difficult task, even for someone named Felicia.

'Look, Peter!' She bent to peer out of the window. 'Isn't Windermere beautiful?'

When she straightened, Peter was staring at her. A deep frown cut his brow.

'I pray that you will be happy here, Felicia. If you are not, I will come straight away and fetch you home.'

She kissed his cheek, half-tempted to return to London this instant.

But only half. A part of her did wonder what life would be like as Viscountess Scarsfeld. Less than a fortnight ago she had seen her future as one where her heart dried out and she became an object of charity.

The truth was, she wanted to give charity, not be the object of it.

'I'll arrange for our bags to be delivered to the hotel,' Peter said while helping her down the train steps.

Felicia ought to be used to the stares by now. Being nearly six feet tall when every other female was so much shorter and having hair so red it would make her velvet hat look as though it might catch fire—well, she did not go unnoticed.

Not that she blamed people for taking a second glance at her. Honestly, Felicia would stare at herself if she saw herself strolling along the other side of the street.

What, she could only wonder, would her fiancé's first reaction to her be? It would be nice if he were not taken aback. In the end it hardly mattered. The pair of them were to be wed, bound by vows for the rest of their lives.

'I wonder why,' she murmured.

'I would prefer not to carry them on my back.'

'Oh, naturally not. But, Peter, why is it so urgent for Lord Scarsfeld to marry, is what I wonder…and wonder. In fact, I have not ceased to dwell on it.'

'All of us have been.' It was true. The Viscount's motives had been discussed for hours on end at Cliverton. 'But I meant what I told you. If you are unhappy, I will come for you.'

'Thank you. Just knowing you will makes this easier. But for all we know he is as pleasant as the star on top of a Christmas tree.'

Or the lump of coal in the bottom of a stocking, was what her cousin's expression answered.

'It was a very long time ago that you encountered him and no doubt he was simply in an ill humour,' Peter said, but she well knew he did not mean it.

Still, she took courage from the white lie because the braver the words, the braver the face, and the easier it was to smile.

'I will meet you at the hotel at half past the hour.' She nodded at the picturesque inn across the road nestled among a grove of bare trees and backed by the blue water of Lake Windermere. 'I see the sweetest gown in the dressmaker's window. Perhaps it can be altered to fit me. I would feel more at ease meeting the Viscount wearing something new.'

Her cousin shifted his gaze to the dress shop and nodded. 'That shade of green suits you. It looks like Christmas.'

Indeed, that was why it had caught her eye. Not only was it the colour of a fresh evergreen, but there were tiny red beads adorning the hem, neckline and ruffled sleeves. The snowflake-hued sash at the waist made it the most cheerful gown she had ever seen.

She would look like a proper peppermint stick—but ever so subtly.

In the end, purchasing the gown took longer than she expected. Peter was no doubt beginning to worry about her.

Coming out of the shop, she sniffed the cold air. The mingled scents of chimney smoke, baked goods from the café next to the dress shop and evergreen trees made her smile.

Lifting her skirts to cross the road, she had a favourable feeling about her future.

She hoped it continued once she met Isaiah Maxwell.

A noise caught her attention. She cocked her head, listening.

Someone was weeping. It sounded like a child, a young girl, perhaps.

This could hardly be ignored. Felicia let go of her

skirt and hurriedly followed the sound along a pathway between the dress shop and the café.

Oh, dear—just there, standing under a tree and gazing up, was a tearful little girl.

Not weeping helplessly, as it had first sounded, but rather in frustration.

'Eloise!' The little girl shook her gloved finger at a cat peering down from a branch. 'Come down at once or I shall leave you to find your own way home!'

Her words were brave, but the tone in which she spoke them indicted her dismay.

'Hello,' Felicia said softly so as not to startle either the girl or her cat. 'I think perhaps I can reach her.'

'Oh, I do hope you can.' The little girl swiped her eyes with her sleeve. 'The silly thing leapt from my basket to go exploring.'

'As a cat will. The ones I have back at home are crafty wee creatures.' Felicia stepped to the base of the tree, slowly lifting her arms, but the cat climbed casually beyond her reach.

'I suppose I will have to summon my brother to climb the tree,' the child muttered with a resigned-looking shrug. Sable lashes narrowed over blue eyes. She shoved a straggling lock of honey-hued hair back under her hat.

'He will not be happy about your antics, mark my word.' She shifted her gaze from the cat, who had paused just out of reach to leisurely groom her tail, to Felicia. 'He told me not to bring her to town, but I did it anyway. Now look what has become of her!'

'He won't be angry, I hope.' She was as unfamiliar with the little boy as she was with the girl who stared at her pet in equal parts worry and annoyance, but she supposed the boy might be upset, given that his wise advice had not been heeded.

'He won't want to be distracted from his errand in order to climb a tree and fetch her down. I do imagine he will be unhappy. My brother is rather accomplished at appearing glum.'

'Let's not trouble him then. I'll climb the tree.'

'Oh, but you mustn't! Not in your skirt. It's far too dangerous. It could tangle and—'

All the more reason it should be Felicia to do it. Little boys were at enough peril on flat ground.

'I'll be right as rain. You need not worry.' Felicia glanced about to make sure they were hidden from view. Satisfied, she bundled up yards of skirt and petticoat, then secured the wad into her waistband as best she could manage. 'I was once adept at chasing cats up trees.'

Of course that had been years ago, but, really, how much could have changed?

'But your shoes? You will need to remove them if you have any hope of not falling.'

'Of course, I was about to do just that.'

She unbuttoned her travelling boots and set them at the base of the tree. Last time she had climbed a tree she had done it barefoot. When one was twelve years old, having unshod feet was acceptable.

The same could not be said for a nearly viscountess. Balancing on branches in stocking feet was sure to be risky, but she could not see any way to avoid it.

So, up she went, grasping rough bark with fingers,

knees and toes. She had not made the second branch before she felt her stocking rip.

What a lucky thing no one was about because her big toe popped boldly into view.

No matter, she was nearly within reach of the cat. It would take but a second to grab it, tuck it into her skirt, then scurry down and put her boots back on.

Goodness gracious, but her feet were cold! Not as cold as her hands, though. They were so frigid she could barely feel what was under her fingertips.

A foot beyond her grasp the cat stared down, languidly swishing her tail.

Chapter Three

Isaiah placed the velvet box containing a wedding band in his pocket, pushing it down deep to be sure it was secure.

He could not recall ever having had such trouble making a purchase. One saw what one wanted and bought it, confident that one's choice was appropriate and pleased to be quickly finished.

This time was different—unsettling, to be honest. The ring was something his bride would wear all her life and he had no idea if she would even like it.

According to the jeweller any woman would adore the warm gold engraved with evergreen needles and dusted with tiny diamonds. Sadly Mr Thompson knew no more about Felicia Merry Penneyjons than Isaiah did.

He would have welcomed Abigail's advice, but she was not here. Mr Thompson had taken one look at Eloise popping out of the basket his sister carried and emitted a room-shattering sneeze.

With the jeweller's eyes growing red and itchy, there

had been no choice but to send his sister to their next stop, the dress shop.

With the wedding set for the day after next, time was of the utmost value. It was vexing to think that the cat might cost him some of it.

As young as she was, he did value his sister's opinion. Females, he had come to learn, had opinions on fashion at a very early age. Her advice on the ring would have been helpful.

He really did want to put his best foot forward for his bride. The woman deserved that respect.

He wondered if perhaps their paths had crossed at a social gathering in the past. It was possible for it to have happened. Now he wished he had paid more than passing courtesy to the ladies presented to him. Had he done that, he might have some idea of who his bride would be.

Stepping outside the jeweller's shop, he shivered. Everything indicated snow was on the way. He would need to hurry if he was to be home before it began to fall.

Hopefully it would not inconvenience Miss Penney-jons.

Isaiah hurried across the street and went inside the dress shop.

Abigail was not there. The shopkeeper shook her head, looking puzzled. Apparently his sister had not arrived.

That could not be! He had watched her cross the road and approach the shop door.

Dashing out of the shop, he pivoted on his heel. Where could she have got to? He felt his skin grow tight, pinched with worry. For all that he tried to smooth his frown before someone noticed, he could not.

Where was she?

Surely she had not become lost. She was familiar with Windermere, every shop and eatery in the village, each street and alley. She knew everyone and they knew her. But she was only eight years old and tourists—strangers from all over—were common.

As if to reinforce his concern a man came out of the hotel, his expression grim. Isaiah reminded himself that just because the fellow scowled while he walked towards the dress shop did not mean it had to do with Abigail. It was unreasonable to think it did.

To say that he was overzealous in protecting his sister would be true, yet he could be no less. On her deathbed his mother had given Abigail to him, trusting that he would keep her safe.

He had failed once when he did not notice that she had toddled outside in a snowstorm. He would never be careless with her safety again.

As soon as he found her he would have a stern, brotherly word with her about caution.

While he thought about what words would best express discipline tempered by love, he heard a screech. It came from behind the dress shop.

Abigail!

On top of Abigail's cry came another. This one seemed to come from a woman.

Skidding on a spot of mud while rounding the corner of the building, he nearly went to his knees.

There was Abigail, her arms spread wide as if to

catch a woman dangling from a tree limb. Even from here he could see the lady's grip slipping.

If she fell, both she and his sister would be injured.

'Stand away!' he shouted on the run.

Abigail jumped aside just in time to avoid being knocked over.

'Let go, miss! I'll catch you!' Feet flailing, she nearly smacked him in the head. As it was, she grazed his hat and sent it flying.

She glanced down, blinking at him with eyes the loveliest shade of green he had ever seen, for all that they were wide with consternation.

Biting her bottom lip, she shook her head fiercely. A lock of red hair lashed her nose. Even in the midst of the crisis he noted that it was softly lustred rather than blazing wildfire.

'You can trust me not to drop you.' Still, she hesitated. 'I promise I will not.'

'He is stronger than he looks,' Abigail explained.

In the next second the lady did tumble, but not, he thought, by choice.

He locked his arms when her weight fell on to him. She gave a small squeak, then stared at him in what could only be surprise.

'You see?' Abigail pointed out. 'Much stronger.'

'I do thank you, sir.'

This was no feather of a miss who would blow away in a breeze. In fact, she filled his arms in such a pleasantly solid fashion, he did not want to put her down.

But he ought to—her bloomers were showing and one long, lovely pink toe peeked out of a rip in her stocking.

'What—' barked a man's voice. Ah, it belonged to the scowling man he'd spotted coming out of the hotel. 'Unhand my cousin! What do you think you are about?'

He would have to, he supposed, the fellow had good reason to be outraged at what he saw.

Setting the lady to her feet, he found that they were of a height, gazing at each other eye to eye. But she was not wearing boots. He imagined when she put them on he would have to adjust his gaze up an inch. The idea intrigued him.

Most women he met were wary of him, of his size and the stern image he tended to present without fully meaning to.

Quite contrary to what his sister had to say, he did not appear a weakling.

'No need to look so surly, Peter,' the lady said, her smile a flash of sunshine on this gloomy day. 'All is well. I was simply fetching the cat out of the tree and I slipped. This kind gentleman caught my fall.'

Eloise chose that moment to claw her way down the tree trunk. With her tail proudly lifted, she sailed across the grass to Abigail, purring and ready to be cooed over.

His sister scooped up the basket from the ground.

'You silly thing,' she gently admonished. Easing Eloise inside, she shut the lid.

This was Isaiah's own fault, he supposed, for not inspecting what she had in the basket when they left Scarsfeld.

'Abigail, did I not instruct you to leave the cat at home?' Perhaps this was best spoken of in private, but the woman might have been injured and he felt his sister ought to apologise. 'Offer your regrets and tell the

lady you are sorry to have involved her in your reck-
less choice.'

'Oh, truly there is no need.' The woman's smile
dimmed. 'No harm was done.'

'Your clothing has been torn. Lady Abigail will find
a way to repay you.'

Glancing down, the lady blushed, yanked the hem
out of her skirt and let it drop, securing her shapely pink
toe from his view.

'Your brother?' she asked Abigail with an inquisi-
tive-looking tilt of her chin.

'You see? It is true what I said.'

'I thought you were speaking of someone much
smaller.' The lady shifted her glance to him, her frown
settling more firmly into place. 'But I do see your point.'

What point?

'Tell the lady you regret having risked her safety
and let's be on our way. I'm certain she would like to
get out of the cold.'

She was not wearing shoes after all and her toe—
dash it, he must put the somehow seductive image of
it from his mind. He was to be wed and thoughts of a
ripped stocking were not appropriate.

'I would.' The cousin shivered, hunching his shoulders against the nip in the air. 'The weather is a bit of
a beast compared to what we left behind in London.'

'I regret that in helping me you were nearly injured.'
Abigail cast him a frown, one which he was fairly certain she had learned from him. 'I also apologise for my
brother's severe attitude. I will suffer no lasting harm
from it, though. Nor will Eloise.'

As if she was suffering even an ounce of harm in the moment. He nearly huffed out loud.

'Naturally not. I'm sure…' In stooping to pick up her shoes, the woman glanced up at him. 'Goodness, I'm only grateful you were close by.'

If his bride was half as lovely as this lady, he would be a thankful man.

Of course, he did not require that his bride be a great beauty. He only prayed that she would be a charming woman who would dissuade Lord Penfield and Lady Penfield from upending Abigail's life.

He squatted, reached for his hat which had come to rest on the heel of her boot. As he gazed at her eye to eye, his stomach took the oddest turn.

An image flashed in his mind, but was gone before he could secure it.

In the instant she grabbed for her shoe, their hands collided. Her bare fingers looked flushed with warmth. He was grateful that he was wearing gloves because to feel the warmth of her skin would twist his belly even further.

He frowned before he could call the gesture back. What a cad he was for getting lost in the colour of her eyes when he ought to have been wondering what his intended's eyes looked like. The situation between him and his bride would be difficult as it was without his interest wandering.

'Have I injured you, sir?' she asked, her voice a horrified whisper.

His dashed frown! Scrubbing it from his face with an open palm, he sent her a smile of reassurance that she had not.

'Oh…' she gasped '…you have been hurt!'

'I have not. As my sister pointed out, I'm stronger than I look.'

The corner of her mouth quirked up. A merry green twinkle flashed in her eye. It was a lucky thing he was squatting because it nearly cut him off at the knees.

'Rest assured, sir, you do not look at all frail.'

He should not ask her name, but rather rise and carry on with purchasing a dress for his sister. The less he knew of this woman the better. As it was, he feared he would imagine her face in moments he ought not to. Which, given his circumstances, would be any moment at all.

'Come along before we freeze,' complained the lady's cousin.

'The weather is lovely, Peter, you simply need to adjust your attitude towards it.'

They were nearly knee to knee when she reached for the package she must have dropped when she went to Abigail's aid. Somehow it felt the most provocative position he had ever been in with a woman, which did not honestly make much sense.

'You'll make an icicle of me, Felicia. Let's be on our way.'

Felicia?

'Felicia?' Surely heaven was smiling upon him.

'Felicia Penneyjons,' she muttered, rising and casting a 'look' at Peter.

Isaiah came to his feet, feeling half-buoyant.

'I'm grateful to—pleased to, that is—meet you.' He took her hand, bent slightly over it. 'I am Lord Scarsfeld.'

* * *

'He's not an ogre, at least,' Felicia muttered to the bedroom at large while dressing for dinner—dinner with Lord Scarsfeld. In her mind, she was not ready to call him Isaiah.

'Not an ogre, perhaps, but as formidable as he was at Lady Newton's ball.'

It surprised her that she had not known him right away when he'd caught her tumbling from the tree. There had been a flash of familiarity, but given the situation she had suddenly landed in—and, well, to be honest, the exceptionally strong arms—she had been so distracted that she had not fully recognised him until he introduced himself.

Something else about the man remained the same. It came to her in the moment she understood who he was. Lord Scarsfeld was still an amazingly handsome man.

She could not deny that looking into his eyes had made her heart flutter. In fact, she wondered if he noticed her fingers trembling a bit when she reached for her boots.

She walked to the mirror, twirled about. She did look like a peppermint stick, but subtly so that only she was likely to know it.

Of course, that was what she intended. While one might wish to feel like a peppermint stick inside, one also wished to appear sensible.

She stopped suddenly, her skirt twirling about her calves.

How sensible, she had to ask herself, was wedding a stranger known to have a less than cheerful disposition? When it came to his sister he was abrupt, even overbearing. But young Lady Abigail had been unfazed by his attitude. She had said what she wished to her brother and about him. If he truly was the man he appeared to be, she would not be so comfortable—bossy, more than that—in his company.

Lord Scarsfeld did confuse her.

Fluffing her skirt, then smoothing her hair, she was determined to sort him out over dinner.

Lady Abigail needed no sorting. Even knowing the child for only a few moments, Felicia liked her immensely. No doubt as the child grew, she would prove equal to society's changes, to the progressive times she would be growing up in.

From what she could determine, her brother had been the one to raise her. In Felicia's opinion he had done an outstanding job.

In the beginning of all this—the summoning of a bride—she had imagined herself playing the role of a martyr to her poor shy sister.

But now...well, having looked into those dramatic, amber-coloured eyes, she was not quite sure she was martyring herself after all. Truly, how many martyrs went to their doom all aflutter over a pair of shapely lips?

None she had ever heard of.

Peter's familiar rap tapped on the door, indicating it was time to go down to the dining room.

Perhaps the flutters had to do with nervousness as much as with a vision of masculine lips and captivating eyes.

Things could be a great deal worse.

Indeed, much worse. Flutters, for whatever their origin, were not a horrid fate. And for all her bravado about offering herself to duty, she had reserved the right to change her mind.

It did seem important to know his reasons for wanting to marry so suddenly after all this time before she committed to it.

Surely he must also have questions for her, such as why she had agreed so readily to the marriage?

She opened the door to find her cousin with a half-smile on his face.

'You are trying to hide the fact that you are worried,' she said, closing the door and taking his arm while they walked towards the stairs.

'Concerned only. You are taking a very big step.' Peter looked her over, at last settling his gaze on her face. 'I'm not sure the two of you will suit.'

'It does remain to be seen, but what we do know is that I am far better suited to Lord Scarsfeld than Ginny would be.'

'You can refuse. I'll take you home this instant.'

'The Viscount and I will dine together. At the end of it I will know if you need to take me home.'

'Very well.'

'And, Peter, I need you to sit at another table. I have questions for Lord Scarsfeld and I wonder if he will answer candidly with you sitting there looking as though you will pummel him at the least provocation.'

Peter huffed out a breath through half-parted lips. 'I'm your guardian. It is suitable for me to appear fierce.'

'You are also a gentleman. Surely you can appear so.'

'Yes, all right. But I will be close by. If you need me, raise your hand in the air, crook your finger and I will come.'

Isaiah would have married any woman and considered himself lucky. It was all for Abigail, after all. Whether the lady was a thistle or a rose, he had prepared himself not to care as long as she was willing to wed him.

Ah, but now, while standing to welcome Miss Penneyjons, watching her willow-like figure as she strode towards him on her cousin's arm, seeing her confident smile when she had every reason to be quaking in her slippers at the prospect of dining with the stranger she had agreed to marry, a stranger his own sister had labelled crusty, he could only admire her.

If she was uncomfortable with gazes shifting her way, she hid it well. Being as tall as she was, she did command attention.

Felicia Merry Penneyjons soaked up every bit of his. To his mind she looked like Christmas.

For an instant the swish of her green skirt, the red beading and white bow at her waist made her appear a walking peppermint stick. A long-dead whisper of Christmas joy echoed in his memory. He sucked in a shallow breath, held it, then snuffed out the feeling before it overwhelmed him.

Christmas joy, the anticipation of something wonderful on the way, all that had died when he was seven years old and his mother had gone away. Without a kiss or a smile, without even a word of farewell, she had vanished from his life.

'Thank you for joining me, Miss Penneyjons, Lord Cliverton.' He nodded in heartfelt welcome while a waiter pulled out a chair for his—his intended was what she was.

Peter shook his head when the waiter went to pull a chair out for him. 'I'll take a table by the window if one is available. The view of the lake is stunning.'

It was, or would be once the sun was shining on it. Being totally dark, the only interest the lake held were a few lights from the opposite shore shimmering through the drizzle.

Isaiah was glad for the empty place at his table. What he wanted was to get to know Felicia. It would be easier with only the two of them making conversation.

'The dining room is lovely,' she said, glancing about the space with a smile.

The woman had an uncommon smile, to be sure. It was pretty, but more than that it made him feel warm inside.

'I dine here often. The food is delicious and there is a beautiful view of the lake when the weather is clear.'

'Everyone does seem to be enjoying themselves.'

'It is cosy with the fireplace burning.'

Humph, if this start to their conversation were any more brittle it would crack.

To prove the point, it did. For a long uncomfortable moment they stared at everything but each other. The silence became embarrassing.

'Do you enjoy it?' she asked at last.

'I do. I find the lamb to be excellent and the wine superb. May I offer you a glass?'

'The rain, I mean. Do you enjoy it? And, yes, a splash of wine would be wonderful.'

'It is a nuisance,' he answered while pouring them each a modest glass. 'I enjoy rain best when it stops.'

For some reason his answer seemed to disappoint her, so he hurried on to another topic. 'My sister sends her thanks for helping to rescue her cat.'

That rallied her smile. 'It's been an awfully long time since I had occasion to climb a tree. But then I don't believe the cat needed rescuing after all. In the end she came down on her own terms.'

'Eloise does live on her own, feline terms, but she is as attached to my sister as Abigail is to her.'

'Your sister seems to be a sweet child and very intelligent to go with it.'

'She's only eight, if you can believe it.'

Silence felled the conversation once more, but this time he nearly saw thoughts swirling past her eyes. She had something she wanted to say, but did not know how to begin.

'Feel free to speak, Miss Penneyjons.'

'Yes, well… I must, mustn't I?' She took a long sip of wine. 'Do you remember us at all? I'm told you and your mother visited Cliverton upon occasion. Also, my sisters and I did encounter you at Lady Newton's ball three years ago.'

'I can't say that I recall meeting you at the ball.'

'I would not expect you to, of course. Ginny and I were only making our debut. A gentleman like you would naturally have his attention focused on the more sophisticated ladies in attendance.'

'May I tell you a secret?' He wanted to smile, but according to Miss Shirls the gesture might frighten her. 'My attention was not on any lady, not that night or on any other. I confess, I am not one for socialising. But there was something, now that I think of it. When you dropped from the tree I had a vague sense of recognising you, but I had no idea from where. Lady Newton's ball must have been it, then.'

'Yes, well, I do tend to be noticed.' She blushed with the confession and for some reason it went straight to his heart, which was odd. When it came to matters of the heart, his was quite dead. 'But, I wonder, do you have any memories of visiting Cliverton? I would not expect you to, really, since you would have been a young boy.'

'Not memories in the usual sense, but I do have a memory of a feeling. I recall a sense of having fun at Cliverton.'

Again, he was struck by her smile. He had to remind himself not to let it affect him in any more than a casual way.

Feeling anything deeper than friendship for anyone but Abigail was not something he was willing to risk. The past had taught him the folly of doing so.

'Well, I'm relieved to hear that.' She took a sip of wine, her lips smiling against the rim of the glass. 'The story that my mother used to tell was that when I was a baby I crawled about after you, wailing and screeching, until you relented and took my hand and helped teach me to walk.'

'Apparently I did a decent job of it. You appear to be agile on your feet. Truly, though, I wish I did remember. No doubt I found you adorable.'

She laughed quietly, pursing her lips in a smile. 'All babies are, of course.'

'For all that they demand every bit of your time and your heart.'

At last, they were speaking easily to one another. It was good to know they could carry on a conversation without tripping all over it.

'Miss Penneyjons, I want to say something—something that cannot be left unsaid.'

'Please Lord Scarsfeld, do speak freely with me. I feel it important that we should be frank with one another.'

'It is simply that I understand you must have given up a great deal in leaving London to come here. I do not take your decision lightly or for granted. You honour me by agreeing to become my wife.'

'Yes, well…in fact, I have yet to give formal approval of the arrangement.'

Had she not? For all that it made sense that she would be cautious, he felt half-sick, fearing she might refuse him. What was he to do if she did?

'What can I do to help you approve? If you have heard things about me, I assure you—'

'I do not pay attention to gossip, my lord. I see with my own eyes that you are not an ogr—' She waved her hand, as if shooing something away. A strand of silky-looking hair escaped confinement, brushing across her ever-so-subtle frown. 'I find it a more reliable habit to form one's own judgements rather than trust someone else's. I promise you that my decision will have nothing to do with anything others might have said about you.'

That was something, at least. The fearful thud of his heart began to ease, the twisting in his gut let up.

'What, then? How can I put your heart at ease?'

'It's my mind more than my heart, I suppose, but what I would like to know is why is it so urgent for you to marry quickly?'

What an uncommon young woman he was going to wed—at least he hoped he was. Some women would not have cared about that, only been content to learn the size, and importance, of his estate.

While he wondered how to begin, he listened to the sounds of silver on china, the quiet murmurs of fellow dinners and the steady tap of rain on the window. His future, and Abigail's, depended upon him presenting his case in the best way.

He was nearly certain she did not want to hear some trite declaration of how he had become weary of being single and that he yearned for the company of a wife. Or of how Scarsfeld needed a viscountess to make it a success in society.

Those reasons were untrue and she would know it.

'It is for Lady Abigail's sake. I must wed if I have any hope of keeping her with me.'

'May I ask why, my lord?'

'It is something you need to know, should you choose in my favour.' He drummed his fingers on the table once then forged ahead. 'My mother died giving birth to Abigail. I was estranged from her and knew nothing of her life, let alone that at forty years old she would— But eight years ago—I was twenty-two then—my late stepfather's solicitor brought Abigail to me in the middle of the night. She was only two days old.'

'It must have come as a horrible shock, finding out about your mother that way.'

'It was horrible. Yet, at the same time, there was Abigail, who is a great blessing.'

'Am I to understand that my purpose in marrying you will be to help you with her?'

'It is more complicated than that, Miss Penneyjons.' Every noise in the room blurred except the increasing tap of rain pelting the windows. 'My sister's uncle, my stepfather's brother, and his wife have decided that she will be better off in London with them. The reason I am in such a hurry to wed is that they are coming to visit for Christmas—they intend to take Abigail with when they leave. My hope is that if I am married they might think me more capable of raising her.'

No one knew any of this, not even the canny Miss Shirls. But Miss Penneyjons did deserve to understand the problem she would be stepping into by accepting his proposal.

'Abigail's uncle and aunt are rather high up in society. As a viscount I would have little chance in court against the Earl of Penfield. My only hope is that if I am respectably married, they will reconsider.'

'Penfield?'

'Are you acquainted with him?'

'No, not really, but being a Londoner I have heard of the Earl and the Countess. I have encountered them briefly in society, although I doubt they would know me. Truly, Lord Scarsfeld, I am very sorry to hear of your trouble. How does Abigail feel about it?'

'She doesn't know.' He scraped his hand across his chin, felt the freshly shaved stubble. 'I can't bring myself to tell her. I'll do whatever is needed to prevent it from happening, as your presence here is proof of.'

'I am taking what you told me to heart.'

'I throw myself upon your mercy,' he whispered and not in jest.

All of a sudden, from one breath to the next, the tapping on the window stopped, which probably meant the rain had turned to snow.

Dash it. He had hoped to make it home before it began to fall.

'Miserable snow,' he muttered. He could only hope that there were a pair of spare rooms to let here at the hotel. The last thing he wanted to do was force his carriage driver to get them home in the slippery mess.

'Surely you do not mean that? Will you escort me outside to see it?' Miss Penneyjons stood up. He suspected she was actually bouncing on the balls of her feet.

He signalled for the waiter to bring their coats. How could he possibly refuse her simple request when he was asking for her life?

In passing by her cousin's table the man looked up, smiling. 'You finally got your snow, Felicia.'

'Isn't it grand?' she answered her cousin, but she was looking at Isaiah.

Judging by her bright smile, she would not care that by going outdoors they would become cold and wet.

'You remind me of Abigail in your love of foul weather,' he pointed out.

'Foul or lovely, it's all in the perception. Snowfall is what it is. It can be miserable or lovely. For me, I choose lovely.'

She was lovely. That was all he could think while he escorted her on to the patio overlooking the lake.

Regrettably, the roof over the terrace kept snow from falling directly on them. Felicia dearly wanted to lift her face and feel icy fingers pat her cheeks, to open her mouth and catch a flake on her tongue.

Since Lord Scarsfeld clearly did not share her joy in being outside, she contented herself with trying to grab the flakes filtering in at them.

For all that she appeared to be having a merry time—appeared to be because she was—she was also deeply considering everything he had told her.

She was grateful he had not flattered her with promises of happy ever after or eventually having an undying love for her.

No, he had trusted her with the truth, confiding his secret. It was going to be a difficult thing to refuse him, if indeed she did.

'Do you wonder, my lord, why I decided to honour our mothers' wishes—to come here and consider your offer? It seems to me it would be important for you to know.'

'I will confess, I have not thought overmuch about it. I was so grateful that you agreed—I am ashamed of that now and I beg your forgiveness.'

'Well, you are in a distressing situation and facing it all on your own. I do forgive you because you ask, even though there is no need to be forgiven anything.'

Isaiah hunched his shoulders against the cold, clearly uncomfortable being out in the elements.

'But why did you come? There are three sisters, are

there not? Were you the only one with the courage to face the ogre?'

'It had nothing to do with courage, at least for me. I've told you how I feel about gossip.'

'Why then?'

'Since you have been honest enough to give me the truth I shall give you the same.' He might not like it, but it was what it was. 'Cornelia, my older sister, is already spoken for. Ginny, the youngest, is terribly shy to the point of being timid. You ought to have seen her face when the news came—oh, well, perhaps you would not have wanted to. She actually does believe gossip. In the event, that left me.'

She shrugged because he could not have failed to be disappointed in her size and her flaming hair. No doubt the thought of being bound to her for ever was daunting.

The only thing to do was to offer him another way out of his problem—because there was one.

'I think you would have been happy had it been Ginny in my place. She is petite and as pretty as a rose and—'

Ginny would be a bride he could be proud to have on his arm. Felicia would clearly be seen as someone Lord Scarsfeld had rescued from the dusty shelf.

'You remind me of a peppermint stick.' Since she could not tell for sure if he was smiling or grimacing, she was hard put to know what he meant by the comment.

'I have no idea if, in your mind, that is a good thing or a bad. I rather like that you think so, though. But there is more to my being here than that I was the only one who would suit. For the one thing, I am a traditional person at heart and feel it only right to respect our parents' wishes. More than that, though, as you surely noticed, I am solidly on the shelf, well on my way to spinsterhood.'

'And marrying me will save you from that?'

'Indeed. I sometimes thought I would not mind it so much. But the fact of it is, when your offer came I was relieved to have a way to avoid that fate.'

'And will you?' He arched a brow. The gesture made him look younger and somehow vulnerable. 'Avoid that fate?'

'Yes…and no.' It cut her to see him look so crestfallen. 'I think I have an idea which will help keep your sister with you, but not bind you to a lifelong marriage.'

To a woman no one else wanted to even dance with.

'It is what I offer you, Miss Penneyjons. My name and my home.'

'But you needn't. At least not for all time. Only until after Christmas and Abigail's aunt and uncle give up their pursuit.'

'For one thing, they might not give up their pursuit. Even if they do…' He shook his head slowly, looking grim. 'At the risk of you turning me down, I will not agree to a temporary marriage.'

He wouldn't? Something in the area of her heart went completely soft. She had offered him an annulment, but in her heart of hearts it was not what she wanted.

'Call me traditional if you like, as you said you were, but I believe marriage is not meant to be temporary, no matter if it is a love match or an arrangement. Vows will be spoken. To me they will be sacred. If you accept me, I offer you all that I have or will have. As far as providing Scarsfeld with an heir, I will not force that upon you. The choice in the degree of intimacy in our marriage will be yours to make.'

Her hair and her face must all look like one great flaming mess.

'You know that I cannot promise undying love—we have only just met.' He took her hand, squeezed her glove. Even through the fabric she felt the heat where they joined. 'What I can and do promise is my undying gratitude.'

Honesty from him was quite a bit more than she had hoped for. Until this afternoon her only hope had been that he would be a bearable man to spend time with.

Lord Scarsfeld, while seeming severe, was honest. Forthright in what he wanted and what he had to offer. In spite of his apparent inability to present a genuine smile, she thought she liked him more than she didn't. And she did genuinely like his sister and cared for her plight.

'There is something—' Isaiah dug about in the pocket of his coat. 'I want to show this to you. Abigail was supposed to help me choose it, but instead she got you stuck up a tree.'

Was that a quirk of a smile at one corner of his mouth?

If it was, she wanted to see more of it. She had the feeling a full grin would banish his vinegary expression at once and expose the man she hoped lived under the mask of severity.

'The truth is I volunteered to go up the tree. I hope you were not—'

While she blundered about saying she hoped he was not too harsh on his sister, he drew the lid off the small box he had taken from his pocket.

Inside was the prettiest gold band she had ever seen. Engraved evergreen branches imbedded with tiny diamonds that looked like a dusting of snow? Had he known her all her life he could have picked nothing she would appreciate more.

With her hand at her throat, she stared at it in silence while fighting a bout of tears.

For a woman who only weeks ago had been resigned to knitting socks in a rocking chair, this moment was overwhelming. To be proposed to with a beautiful ring—she could never have imagined such a thing would happen to her.

'If you don't like it, we can choose another together.'

'It is the most perfect ring I have ever seen.' She closed the lid because looking at it one more moment would make her weep out loud.

'But you are turning me down?' He slid the box back in his pocket. 'It's all right, Felicia. I know I asked a great deal. I wish I could accept your offer of an annulment, but I cannot.'

'I didn't want one. I only thought it the right thing to do. And I am not turning you down.' She moved to swipe away a tear , but he caught her glove.

'Are you truly willing? It's not my intention to offer you a trap.'

'I'm a good bit more willing than I expected to be,

if you want the truth.' If she did not wipe that tear, it would drip off her nose.

'We will face challenges, Felicia. You will more than I, but I promise to be the best man I can be.'

Saying that, he leaned forward, lifted his lips a scant inch and kissed the tear away.

Chapter Four

Sitting in the rented carriage, Felicia opened the window to let fresh cold air nip her face. She breathed in the scent of Lake Windermere, then took a deeper breath of fresh spruce which made her long for everything Christmas.

She was on her way to Scarsfeld, on her way to the rest of her life, whatever it turned out to be.

The fact that it did not involve long lonely hours in a rocker, clicking knitting needles and napping, told her she had chosen wisely in agreeing to wed Lord Scarsfeld.

More than that, the fact that she still felt his lips on her cheek hinted that she had made a very good—

'This is a mistake, Felicia. It sends a chill up my neck. We were in town only a short while and I heard people speaking ill of the man.'

'What kind of ill?'

'They say he is sullen and joyless. I do not think he will suit you.'

'Idle tongues… I am surprised you listened to them.'

Resigned to the fact that her happy moment of gazing out the window was at an end, she closed it and turned her attention to her cousin.

'You ought to look for good in all things, Peter.'

'That is exactly my point. You see it even when it ought not to be. I fear you see everything through rose-tinted spectacles.'

'Why is it that I feel somehow insulted?'

'Insulting you was not my intention, only to make you look at this situation clearly. You will not be happy with the man, in my opinion. You need a more cheerful fellow.'

'It is not your cheek he kissed,' she mumbled.

'What was that?'

'Never mind.' She doubted that Peter had deliberately cast doubt upon her ability to make a sound decision. Rose-tinted spectacles, indeed. 'Just because I choose to cast a positive light on people…and circumstances…does not limit my ability to make a sensible decision for my future.'

And for young Abigail's.

Let her cousin doubt her. She was not going to reveal Lord Scarsfeld's secrets. No matter how feather-witted her cousin thought her to be, she would remain silent on her intended's reasons for marrying.

'You accuse me of looking through rose-tinted spectacles while all the while you are wearing blinkers. The Viscount has made me a respectable proposal of marriage. My mother would have approved of it and so do I.'

'But why, for pity's sake?'

'Because one day you will marry, my sisters will,

too. You will have children. I have no wish to be their burdensome maiden aunt.'

'Any one of us would be happy to take you into our homes.'

'I know that…but I would not be happy. I would wake up every morning wondering how much pity I could endure.' She reached across, squeezed Peter's hand. 'I only want what any other woman does.'

'I don't know any other woman who would want it with Lord Scarsfeld.'

'That is because they have not felt him kiss their cheek.' This time she said it plainly.

'What?' Peter's jaw fell open. In her mind she saw it hit his knees. It was not easy to withhold a giggle. 'He did that?'

'Indeed. It was quite sweet considering he is an ogre. I was crying and so he kissed the tear away.'

'He made you weep! And you have yet to say your vows! Now I know you are not thinking clearly.'

'I was weeping because he was truthful with me in his reasons for wishing to marry, which I will not share with you. And because he nearly smiled. I'm certain I saw the man beneath the frown in that moment.' And here she was, ready to weep again just remembering. 'But mostly he gave me something I never dared hope for—a heartfelt wedding proposal. And wait until you see my wedding ring. He chose it himself. Really, it could not be more perfect had I designed it. Honestly, Peter, I never dreamed a woman like me would ever have that moment.'

Her cousin blinked at her in silence. Of course he was a man and might not understand.

'And he did not have to stand on a stool to kiss my cheek.'

'There is that, I suppose. If you are certain… I support your decision.'

'Thank you.'

Her cousin was a very good man. He had been only twenty when he became Cliverton and took over the care of her and her sisters. It was no wonder he was protective of them. Playmates turned suddenly into girls to be watched over. It could not have been easy for him.

'Do you remember what we spoke about on the train?' she asked.

'Some of it.'

'The part about me having a purpose? I wonder if it is my purpose to bring happiness to Lord Scarsfeld's life?'

'I wonder if you might have just as easily found your purpose at home, but I did say I support you so I will not speak of it again.'

'No one at Cliverton really needs me. But here… I think perhaps they do.'

Because she had caught a glimpse of the man Lord Scarsfeld kept hidden, she hoped she could give him what he needed. And not only with regard to his sister's situation.

A challenge had been set before her and she felt a thrill at rising to it.

'And I said, if anyone could make the Viscount happy it would be you.'

'You see? I have not made a mistake. I am fulfilling a higher purpose.'

A rap tapped smartly on the roof. Peter rolled down the window and peered up at the driver.

'Scarsfeld Manor just ahead sir.'

Settling back, Peter crossed his arms over his chest, then simply stared at her.

'I pray that no one ever takes away your rose-tinted spectacles, Felicia. The world is a better place for you wearing them.'

She did not know about the world. She only hoped to make her new home a better place. That she would be able to help convince Lord and Lady Penfield that Lady Abigail was better off being brought up where she was.

Isaiah stared out of the conservatory windows, his attention on the half-mile view of the road leading to the estate. He had been doing this on and off all morning. Now that it was nearing one in the afternoon, it was more on than off.

Surely any moment he would see a hired carriage coming from the village. His offer to send the Scarsfeld coach to bring Felicia here had been rebuffed by her cousin.

No doubt it was because Lord Cliverton hoped Felicia would change her mind and return to London.

Watching the expanse of white where nothing moved except a half-hearted breeze plopping snow from tree branches, he wondered if she had changed her mind.

Looking back, he probably should not have kissed her cheek. Her tears were her own business and it had been forward of him to take them upon himself.

Of course, women's tears had always been a difficult thing for him to see. Ever since that Christmas morning when, before dawn, his mother had shaken him from sleep and, weeping, informed him they were going away to live in London with her new husband. Being as young as he was, he hadn't understood what it all meant—nor had he foreseen what was coming for him and his young, beautiful mother. The only question he really had had for her in the moment was how Father Christmas would find him.

He had often wondered over the years why his stepfather had chosen Christmas morning to rip them from home. Pure nastiness was all he had ever been able to come up with.

Try as he might, he had never been able to forget the worst of that morning. In memory it was as horribly vivid as the moment it happened.

In passing the Christmas tree, he had caught sight of the small gift he had spent the autumn making. It was a necklace made from birch wood which the stableman had helped him create.

Wriggling free of his mother's grip, he ran to get it. A bony-fisted hand caught the collar of his nightshirt, yanked him off his feet, then hauled him towards the front door.

'You'll make us late.' His new stepfather had a stern voice that used to frighten him. 'And put away your snivelling, boy. Act like the Viscount you will become one day.'

His mother made an attempt to point out he was only a child, but her husband said something—he could not recall the words—only how hurtful they were and how his mother wept even harder.

Oddly, what stood out after everything had settled was how beautiful the tree looked in the dim light of the parlour. Even in the midst of his tragedy, it sparkled mockingly in the moonlight streaming in the window.

Shaking off visions of the past, he returned to watching the road, praying Felicia Penneyjons had not changed her mind.

If she had, what would he do? There was no time to find another bride. Besides, he liked Miss Penneyjons— had thoroughly enjoyed the slice of a moment his lips lingered on her cheek.

Closing his eyes, he prayed that Miss Penneyjons would keep her word, come to Scarsfeld and be his bride because no matter what, he was not going to allow his sister to be ripped from her home the way he had been.

'Amen,' he whispered, then opened his eyes.

And just there, turning on to the drive, was a carriage.

'Amen and thank you,' he whispered, rushing into the house and summoning the household to present a proper greeting to the future Lady Scarsfeld.

'It's not what I expected.' Peter's whisper was low enough that Felicia was confident the staff, lined up on either side of the hall, could not hear what he said.

'What did you expect?' she whispered back.

For Felicia's part, she had not thought to see the most appealing room she had ever entered.

It was elegant, but not in a stuffy way. With its walls and grand stairway polished so well the wood looked warm to the touch, with the cheerful rug in shades of orange, yellow and red, along with the huge stone fireplace that suffused everything in a welcome glow—

well, she could only wonder if this room reflected a part of Lord Scarsfeld's character that he did not express.

'Something more severe, I suppose—more like him.'

'You do not know him well enough to make such a judgement.'

'I am about to—here he comes.'

Lord Scarsfeld strode into the room, young Lady Abigail walking beside him. They stood at the head of the line of servants.

Abigail tugged on her brother's sleeve, then whispered something in his ear. He grimaced, which made Abigail shake her head and frown.

With that, the pair of them made their way towards her and Peter. Luckily Abigail's smile was full of welcome because her brother's seemed rather pinched.

Which was understandable, Felicia thought. Proposing marriage so suddenly to a stranger was a rash thing to do. But not, perhaps, as rash as accepting said stranger's offer.

No doubt her answering smile was pinched at the corners, too.

'Welcome to Scarsfeld, Miss Penneyjons.'

'You have a beautiful home,' she answered, then she nodded to her soon-to-be little sister. 'It is good to see you again, Lady Abigail. I trust your cat is faring well after her adventure in town?'

'She was in a bit of a mood from having been stuffed in the basket for so long, but she has recovered.' Evidently this was true since at that moment the cat was happily twining herself about the butler's ankles. 'Welcome to Scarsfeld, Miss Penneyjons. I hope you will be happy here with us.'

'How could I not be with a new sister to become acquainted with?'

She walked down the line of servants next to Lord Scarsfeld as he introduced her to the staff. She greeted each person, complimenting them on maintaining such a lovely house.

Having accepted their good wishes, she knew there was no going back now. Even before taking her vows, she had stepped into her role as mistress of Scarsfeld.

Funny that she was excited about it more than frightened.

Of course she had not been named Lady 'Woebegone' or Violet, as in shrinking.

And tomorrow she would become Lady Scarsfeld—Felicia Merry Scarsfeld, for better or for worse.

Teatime passed pleasantly enough with Isaiah's soon-to-be family, but now it was time to show off Scarsfeld to its new mistress.

He prayed she would like it. He had very little to offer her in this marriage other than this grand and lovely home, his title and his wealth. All things which some women would be contented with, but he suspected Miss Penneyjons wanted more.

What he could not give her was what a wife had a right to expect from her husband. The part of his soul capable of loving deeply was dead, killed by his mother, the one person who ought to have loved him most.

No woman he had ever met—other than Abigail—had been able to convince him that loving was worth the risk.

It might not be right, but friendship was all he had to offer his bride.

'May I show all of you the house?' he asked in order to be polite, but he hoped it would be him and Felicia, alone.

'I've seen it,' Abigail declared while picking up one of the special teacakes Cook had prepared for guests. Which meant she did not prepare them all that often. 'I'll take this one for my nanny, Miss Shirls. Maybe it will sweeten her and she will let me choose the book for our afternoon reading.'

Abigail skipped out of the room. Watching her go, Isaiah could not help but smile inside. He knew well that the scone would not last halfway up the stairs.

'My sister reads whatever she pleases as soon as Miss Shirls dozes off in her chair.'

Peter patted his stomach. 'Perhaps I will go exploring later. A doze sounds just the thing.' With that he stood, bent to kiss Felicia's cheek, then departed for one of the guest rooms.

'I would enjoy a tour.'

Felicia's voice startled Isaiah. Apparently he had lost himself, staring at the spot Peter so casually kissed. The previous night when Isaiah had kissed her cheek it had not been a casual gesture, done then forgotten. Oddly, it still lingered in his mind, had poked at his heart ever since.

While tender affections towards this woman were to be expected and completely appropriate up to a point, he reminded himself that the closest of attachments could be broken, leaving lives shattered.

Felicia had offered him a way to avoid risking heartache. No one would invest themselves in a temporary match.

Which did nothing to change the fact right was right and wrong was wrong: vows made were vows kept.

So here he was, showing Miss Penneyjons her new home. What he needed to keep in mind was that if a mother could leave her child, then—

It would be wise not to give Miss Penneyjons any more of himself than was required of a friendly marital union.

If he ended up losing Abigail, he would be shattered beyond bearing. To also risk such a thing with Miss Penneyjons? No, he could not.

'Shall we begin down below in the kitchen and work our way up?'

'The kitchen is one of my favourite places in a home. It is warm no matter the time of day or night and it always smells so good. Although, our cook in London does not like us underfoot and shoos us out.'

'You will be happy to know that Mrs Muldoon enjoys showing off her skills and does not mind being watched.'

He used to do that. As an adolescent he was hungry all the time. Mrs Muldoon let him sit on a kitchen stool while she fed him. She had also talked to him because she understood that he craved company as much as he craved food.

After visiting the kitchen, he took Felicia to the library, then the vast ballroom that was not used for anything.

'I'd like to know more about you, my lord, since we are about to undertake a task of great urgency.'

Urgency was an odd way to refer to being joined in marriage. Which did not mean it was incorrect.

He could not help feeling shamed. She was giving him so much—her life, in fact—and he was offering her marriage with no intention of giving her his heart.

'Have you lived here all your life?'

'Most of it. I was born here, but my father died when I was a few weeks old. Until I was four years old it was only Mother and me.'

An echo of long-vanished laughter washed over the ballroom, his babyish, his mother's joyful as she chased after him while he dashed madly about on his small German scooter.

'But when my mother remarried I went with her to live at Penfield. I was sent back after a few years. Lord Penfield decided Scarsfeld was where I belonged, given I was the Viscount. But I suspect he wanted to be rid of a child who was not his own. As young as I was, I knew he did not want to share my mother's attention with anyone.'

For many years this house and the servants who came and went had been his only family. These old walls, the only witness to the times he had frolicked with his mother, rolling on the floor while being tickled and cuddled—of the times he had fallen into sweet dreams snuggled on her lap.

Loss was a bitter thing and better not dwelt upon. He did his best not to think of those days. But they were there, lurking in the shadows of his mind. Especially now that he faced the threat of Abigail being ripped from her home—from him.

Ah, but here was his future, looking at him with her lips pressed and a frown dipping her brows.

'I imagine it sounds grim. The truth was, I missed Scarsfeld and was happy to be home.' It wasn't all of the truth, but he said so to put Felicia at ease. 'Come, let us go to the conservatory and you can tell me about your childhood.'

He led the way, listening to the rustle of her skirts as she followed.

'Life at Cliverton has always been noisy. You will recall that I have two sisters, but my parents also brought up Peter. My poor cousin, with three girls there was always someone crying over this or that, always yards of fabric draped everywhere because girls are in constant need of new dresses. Of course, there was far more laughter than tears, but naturally Peter, being the only boy, did not find it amusing. Being a big brother to three girls had to have put a strain on him.'

'I can imagine. I have only one and she is a challenge.'

'Yet she is the light of your life. I saw the way you smiled at her when she ran off with the teacake.'

'My sister was up to mischief. I did not smile.'

'Perhaps you did not in the normal way, with your lips. But I saw it in your eyes, Lord Scarsfeld. Your smile was as doting a one as I have ever seen.'

As far as he knew no one had ever looked close enough to see what lay beyond his habitual frown—to who he was underneath it. This pleased him—but it frightened him more.

'But you are correct, she is the light of my life. If I have any hope of keeping her, I will owe it to you.'

'Don't worry, Isaiah, when Lord and Lady Penfield come they will see how happy Abigail is and they will not have the heart to disrupt her life.'

Hearing her use his given name caused something warm to roll through his chest—something odd and curious.

He opened the conservatory door. It was chilly in here, but not nearly as frigid as it was outside.

'We keep a fire going here at all hours,' he explained. 'Even though it is still chilly, I prefer to have Abigail play inside. It is much safer here than out there in the freezing temperatures.'

He watched Felicia walk to the window and touch the glass with her fingertips.

She was silent for so long—what was she thinking? That the view was forbidding at this time of year? That she disliked it?

'It is beautiful in the spring and summer,' he said.

'I imagine it is spectacular in autumn as well. But winter! It looks like a fairyland out there. I half expect to see a snow queen skating past, tapping the lake surface with her wand and turning it to ice ahead of her.'

Felicia spun about, her smile so bright and engaging that he half wondered if a snow queen might actually glide past.

'If one could step into a fantasy world, I rather think I would enjoy being a snow queen, all a-sparkle and glittering.'

'It would need to be a fantasy since the lake rarely freezes solid enough to be skated upon.'

She crooked her finger, beckoning him join her at the window.

'Come,' she said, standing so close that their shoulders nearly touched. 'You can be my snow king, King Snowfeld, mighty enough to freeze a volcano.'

She pointed to the furthest visible point of the lake. He ought to be looking where she directed, but her hand was so fair, her finger long, lovely and slender. He could look no further than that.

'Ah, there you are, covering the ice with such powerful speed that ice and sparks are flying from the blades of your skates. You are an impressive sight, to be sure. I'm not frightened of you, though. You and I often skate together and have the best time. Look, you just picked me up and sailed past this window. It looks as if I am flying, does it not?'

'I see us falling through the ice, never to be heard from again.' While he hated to burst her pretty scene, he was not a powerful snow king and if the lake did freeze, it would still be too dangerous to skate on.

'In the real world naturally one would not venture out on it.' She shrugged. It startled him to note that their shoulders were no longer nearly touching, but pressed together, arm to elbow. 'I'm sorry, I should have remembered that fantasy scenes are better indulged in with one's sisters. Peter was always driven to distraction when we tried to include him. It's only that the view from this room is incredibly beautiful. I got carried away and I apologise.'

The last thing she ought to be doing was apologising to him. A grateful man would have gone along with her little story, told her how holding her aloft made him feel as if he was flying with her.

'Yes, well—were I half the man as the King Snowfeld I… I would…twirl you about in a grand way… and—'

'It's all right, my lord. You need not play a game which goes against your nature. But it was kind of you to attempt it.'

'There is one thing I would do if I were Snow King.'

'Truly?' Somehow her smile made the world beyond the window seem less bleak. He had never seen a smile that could do that. 'What is it?'

'I would command you to call me Isaiah and to think of me as a friend.' He would have said husband, but that word implied an intimacy neither of them felt. A friendly husband was more what he was. 'An ally.'

'I will call you by your name as long as you return the favour and call me Felicia. And you are correct. We are allies in the cause of keeping Abigail at home.'

Allies, but she had not added friend. He could hardly blame her for leaving that word out. Friends had fun together. As far as he knew, the only one who considered him fun was Abigail.

'You have a very nice name, Isaiah. I shall enjoy using it. But do you have a middle name?'

'I do, but it is an odd one. Only a few people know it.' Because it was not only odd, it was downright strange. 'It is Elphalet.'

'Isaiah Elphalet.' She repeated it again. 'Do you know what it means?'

'It means that I keep it to myself.'

'Well, I thank you for sharing it with me. Did you know that names are meaningful? Have no fear, Isaiah, we shall get to the bottom of yours.'

Fear learning the meaning of his name? Of all the

things he feared, that was not one he had ever considered.

However, he was beginning to fear the warm 'something' that stirred in his chest when he looked at her. He did fear that.

He had never allowed that depth of affection for anyone but his sister. He had never even allowed himself to fall in love.

It was safer not to, yet looking back over the lonely years made him feel as cold as if he had fallen into frigid Lake Windermere.

Chapter Five

It was not uncommon for a bride to be restless on the night before her wedding, even if it was a small, intimate affair like hers was bound to be, Felicia thought while coming out of the library in the wee hours with a book hugged to her chest.

For many brides it would be the anticipation of the wedding night keeping them restless. Apparently she had nothing to fear on that count.

That was something at least, was it not?

Walking from the cold dark library towards the kitchen, which was certain to be warm at any hour, she thought about what a puzzle her soon-to-be husband was.

Clearly he had been wounded by his childhood and deeply.

She had tested him earlier when he'd shown her the conservatory, inviting him to join her in the King Snowfeld game. She wanted to know how deeply his past had scarred him.

Her strategy had not revealed it quite yet, but at least

he had tried to join her in the fun. As awkward as the attempt had been, it had touched her because it indicated that he did care that she be content living at Scarsfeld.

And truly, she did want to be happy. In order for that to happen she needed to discover what her purpose here would be. There was Abigail's plight to be sure, but beyond that? Once the child's security was established, what was there for Felicia to do?

Surely it would become clear in time, would it not? For now she would keep her mind entertained by reading the book she had clutched to the lapels of her robe.

She needed something to keep her mind from entertaining sad thoughts—such as her sisters being unable to attend her wedding. For years they had played at it, dressing up in fancy clothing and marching down the aisle. Not once had they dreamed of doing it without one another.

But more than that, she missed Mama. Ten years ago when the accident had taken her parents, she, Peter and her sisters had needed to fight their way back from Hades. Poor Peter, he had borne the weight of it, becoming Cliverton at only twenty years old. But they had fought their way back and found new life—joyful life, as Mama and Papa would have wanted.

Well, now here she was on the eve of her wedding and she wanted her mother.

What she needed to remember was that she was doing exactly what Mama had wanted. Surely her mother was with her in whatever mysterious way she could be?

Maybe her book could provide her with some distraction.

* * *

At this quiet hour no one was in the kitchen, but the space was still warm. The scent of freshly baked bread lingered in the air.

She lit a small lamp and set it on the table top which formed something of an island in the middle of the room.

Tea would be lovely so she made a cup. Oh, and just there under a cloth were cakes left over from the previous day's afternoon tea.

She pulled over a chair and settled upon it. This was far more pleasant than pacing her chamber floor, feeling dizzy with all the emotions swirling inside her.

Opening the book of name meanings, she flipped the pages to the name 'Isaiah.'

Hmm… Apparently there were many ways to spell the name.

'I-S-A-I-A-H,' she spoke the letters aloud. This was how her intended spelled it. Of all the spellings she liked this one best.

Sipping tea and then nibbling a corner of the cake, she looked over the meanings of his name. There were a few to choose from, but they all came down to one.

'The Lord saves,' she read out loud, not sure how it applied to her Isaiah.

Oh. She dropped the cake in scrambling to keep hold of the teacup. Why had she referred to him as 'her Isaiah,' even in the privacy of her mind?

Because—well, it must be that he was about to become her husband and she his wife. The very nature of the union made them each other's.

She shook her head. She had thought of him as hers

and no matter how long she stared at the cake she held in her fingers, trying to figure out why, she had done it, there was no changing the thought.

Elphalet. She redirected her attention to Isaiah's middle name.

'God has judged?' She set the teacup down, propped her chin in one hand then nibbled the cake. 'That hardly helps.'

'It would be quite unfortunate if one were found lacking,' came a voice from the shadowed doorway. 'What are you doing down here in the middle of the night?' Isaiah asked, stepping fully into the circle of lamplight.

What? She knew what she had been doing. But now? In this instant?

Well, she was staring at him, was what she was now doing. His hair was all—loose, the curls wild and tumbled looking. Not only that, the front of his robe gaped open and she caught a glimpse of his skin under the soft-looking flannel, skin that would normally go unseen. No doubt he expected to be alone this time of night.

What was she doing, indeed?

'I could not sleep so I decided to research the meaning of your name.'

He pulled a chair out and sat across from her.

'What did you discover?'

'That you are a mystery.' She broke the cake and gave half of it to him. 'Even a contradiction.'

'How so? And thank you.'

'Well, you see, we have "Isaiah." That means "The Lord saves." Which is lovely, but then it is complicated by Elphalet. There we have "God has judged," and as you pointed out, that would be unfortunate if one were found lacking.'

'I suggest we should leave it at "God has judged mercifully and saved." But tell me, Felicia, why are you so restless that you are in the kitchen at—' he glanced about '—whatever time it is?'

'No doubt it is for the same reason that you are.' There was a crumb at the corner of his mouth. She wished it would fall off so that she would not have to resist the temptation to wipe it away. Had she been any other nearly bride she would have done it without a thought. 'Our wedding is tomorrow.'

'Are you now regretting it?'

For pity's sake! The crumb did fall, but it teetered on the lapel of his robe, right where the fabric crossed into a V shape. At this point it could either travel to his lap, or slip inside his robe and go—oh, never mind. She was not that kind of bride.

'I do not think so. Are you?'

'No, Felicia. I am not regretting it.' He reached across the table and covered her hand with his. What a warm and friendly gesture. 'I find you to be lovely and charming.'

He did?

She indicated the unkempt mass of her hair by lifting her brows towards it. She did not want to point to her head and lose the warm contact of his fingers.

'There is something I cannot help but wonder, Isaiah,' and it was not what his hand would feel like touching, oh, say her hair or her lips. 'I do wonder what you will want of me once your sister is secure here at home. What will my purpose at Scarsfeld be?'

'It can be whatever you choose it to be.'

'Honestly, Isaiah, that is rather vague. What does that even mean? I could swing about in the conservatory like a circus performer and you would not mind?'

'Perhaps I would mind that.'

What was that? She could not be certain in the dim light, but she thought, just perhaps, he smiled—with his mouth.

Was that to be her purpose? To make him smile? She had wondered about it, but really, that was a goal more than a purpose.

'Abigail will need you, of course. She has been too long without a woman to guide her. Miss Shirls is devoted to her, but she cannot guide her in the ways of proper society.'

All right, yes, she would enjoy helping Abigail, being a big sister to her. Not for social guidance only, which was important for a young lady, but also to show her how to have girlish fun. That was every bit as important and it was unlikely that she would learn it from her brother or her nanny.

Whereas Felicia excelled at having fun.

'Will you not hire a governess?'

'I intend to at the beginning of next year. But at the moment I am preoccupied with keeping my sister with me. If we succeed, then I will find a governess.'

'We will succeed. Never doubt it.'

It sounded a good thing to say even though she did have a rather strong dose of doubt. But right at this moment her purpose was to encourage him.

They were silent for a while. No doubt they were

each trying to convince themselves that what she had just said was true.

'There is something about our marriage I must speak of—'

'Please do speak freely, Isaiah.'

He cleared his throat. 'As time goes by…when you get to know me and I you—you might find that you want—'

Good heavens! Isaiah Maxwell, the fearsome Lord Scarsfeld, was blushing. Even in the dim light she could clearly see the flush heating his cheeks.

'To give you an heir?' she supplied. No doubt she was blushing as furiously as he was.

What a pair they were. Her lungs hitched, a giggle escaping even though the subject they were discussing was a serious one. But really, the sight of two people blushing at each other on the night before their marriage was simply funny.

'Yes, but as I told you before, the choice is yours alone.'

'Is it really? I rather think it is a decision to be made by two people.'

'I only meant that—' She had to wonder if he noticed he was still holding her hand. Since she was enjoying the contact she would not point it out. 'As you have not had much choice in any of this, I feel you ought to have that one.'

'You are wrong in that, Isaiah. I did have a choice.' She turned her hand so that her fingers entwined with his. 'I made it and here I am.'

He closed his eyes, as if blinking, but left them closed for a long time. Then when he opened them, she thought—but of course she must be mistaken—that it was moisture he had been blinking away.

Lifting her hand, he drew it towards him, kissed her knuckles and then let go.

'There are no words to express my gratitude. Abigail would feel the same if she knew.'

'It is better that she does not know, I think. You made the right choice in not telling her. Why should she need to worry, especially with Christmas at hand?'

'It is good to have an ally. I can't recall ever having had one before.'

'Yes, well, you have never had a wife before. The very nature of the relationship calls for it.'

'I like you, Felicia.'

'I like you, too.'

'Is there anything I can say, any question you might have about tomorrow that I can answer to help you get some rest?'

'I do have one.' There she was, blushing again, but she really did want to know this one thing. Any bride would. 'Are you going to kiss me? After the vows are finished, do you plan to kiss me? If you don't want to, I understand, but—well—I just want to know what to expect.'

He stood up. The crumb fell into the robe. Where had it gone—never mind. She had been too forward already without adding that crumb to her sins.

'Would you welcome it if I did?'

The truth was the truth and there would be nothing to gain by denying it.

Her throat went tight and dry all of a sudden so her only answer was a jerky nod.

'Expect this, then.'

With that he leaned across kitchen table, bent and placed his lips on hers. The pressure was so light and brief that it might have been a hot breeze passing between them.

At ten in the morning on his wedding day, Isaiah stared at the grand stairway. From his position in front of the parlour window he had a clear view of the steps down which his bride would descend.

This wedding was not quite what he had imagined it would be—or, more correctly, the bride and his feelings about her were not what he imagined they would be.

At the start of his grand scheme, his fantasy wife was no more than a convenient means to an end. It had not mattered to him who she was. Either Felicia or Ginny—or any lady willing to come north and wed him at short notice—would have suited.

What a fool he had been to not understand that a wife would be more than a guest in his home.

Having known Felicia for little more than two days, he understood how wrong, how shallow, his thinking had been.

Clearly Felicia was not a lady to quietly take her place in the background of his life. He feared that she would become a flame to the brooding corners of his heart, lighting them one by one until he was as exposed, as broken as the little boy he had been when his mother had left him.

Somehow he could not shake the worry that even now Felicia might wish to flee from him—might reconsider her decision to wed him.

With everyone in their appointed places—the vicar on one side of him, Peter on the other and Miss Shirls standing next to the vicar's wife—Isaiah was the one who felt an odd urge to flee.

His heart pounded and, as unmanly as it seemed, his knees were nearly knocking.

Felicia ought to be coming down the stairs by now. It was ten minutes past the appointed time.

What if she really had changed her mind?

What if the kiss he had given her last night, as brief as it was, had displeased her? He hadn't meant to give it, but she was just so pretty sitting in the dim light of the kitchen, gazing up at him in expectation with that shy little smile on her face. Dash it, her lips had been glistening in the lamplight.

'If I were Miss Penneyjons, I would not come down.' Miss Shirls appeared suddenly at his elbow, glancing about the room and wagging her head. 'You, my lord, have made a mess of this.'

'I have no idea what you mean.' He did not since she could not be referring to last night. She could not mean his appearance since he was wearing his best suit and his boots were polished to a shine.

'Truly you do not? Where are the flowers? Where is the small orchestra for my lady to make her entrance to? Even a small wedding requires them.'

He heard the reverend clear his throat and saw him glance at the clock.

He vaguely recalled Miss Shirls mentioning those things were expected, but he had been distracted with all that was going on and not given frills their apparent importance.

He wished he had paid closer attention to her because now here he stood, feeling ashamed of his neglect.

He was not even a husband yet and already he had failed.

In a few more moments he was going to fail again.

Last night in the warm glow of the kitchen, in the warmer glow of Felicia's presence and talk of their future, he had promised to kiss his bride again—that the first one had been a mere foretaste of what was to come. At the time it had seemed right and natural.

But now? He could not be certain what the brief, light kiss had meant to her, but he did know what it meant to him.

Far too much. It had shaken him to the point that he began to feel things he did not want to feel, stirrings in his heart better left unstirred.

He greatly feared he could not kiss her again without giving a part of himself away that he had no wish to give.

Miss Shirls went back to her place beside the vicar's wife. They chatted quietly under their breaths.

Not so quietly that he could not catch a phrase or two. They wondered if he had even provided a bouquet of flowers for his bride to carry.

The ladies were about to discover he had not. No doubt they would conclude he would be a less than stellar husband.

He feared they were not wrong. But for a far more serious reason than failing to provide pretty decor.

Here he stood, on the verge of taking the most lovely of women to be his wife, yet had no intention of allowing her too deeply into his heart.

Guilt stabbed him right in the gut because, in spite of what Felicia believed, any man would be lucky to have her. Another man would have thought to give her flowers and music which would be a token of respect she deserved on her wedding day.

Another man could have given her not only respect, but deep affection. But his heart was damaged and so he could not offer her that, if, in fact, she even wanted his heart.

In spite of that—and the doubt and the nagging feeling that Felicia deserved better than anything he could give—it did not change the fact that Abigail's future might depend upon this marriage.

Isaiah watched the stairs, listening for the creak of footsteps from upstairs and wondering, again, if she had changed her mind.

How long was it proper to wait before sending someone up to see if she intended to come down?

As long as it took for the vicar to gather his wife and go home, was how long. He would not move from this spot until then.

Funny, he had never noticed how loud the clock ticked. It sounded like a drumbeat, more ominous than the wind whispering at the windowpane.

Abigail rushed into Felicia's chamber, out of breath.

'I found it!' She clutched a bouquet of holly and bright red berries tied up in red and white ribbons. 'It was not where my brother told me it would be, so I had to hunt high and low for it.'

'It is so beautiful. Perfect for a December wedding.' Felicia took the bouquet from her future sister.

'He made it himself, with his own hands.'

The maid who had helped her dress and styled her hair into lovely curls slapped her hand over her mouth, then spun towards the window.

Apparently the maid found the idea of Lord Scarsfeld doing such a thing as unlikely as Felicia did.

'He made a beautiful job of it,' Felicia said. 'I've never seen anything so pretty. How thoughtful it was for him to think of it.'

'Oh, my brother is often thoughtful.'

Hmm... Abigail's cheeks were flushed as if she had just run in from the cold. The stems of the holly felt chilled. There was no doubt about who the thoughtful one was.

Looking at Abigail's happy expression, knowing what she would do to save face for her brother—or perhaps to do what she could to please Felicia—she knew she was making the right choice in going down the stairs to wed a puzzle of a stranger.

Given what Isaiah was willing to do in order to protect his sister, he must have a loving heart. Felicia was convinced that there was more to him than the severe image he portrayed. Indeed, last night she'd had a glimpse of it—a taste of something she might want more of.

All right, she was ready for this.

She reached for Abigail's hand. Together they went out of the room and stood at the top of the stairs.

The sound of feet shuffling into place below made her heart slam against her ribs.

It was so very quiet down there, not a note of music to mark her descent down the stairs. Apparently the wind whistling about the house was to be her wedding march.

But wait—a voice came drifting from the parlour. Deep and masculine, it drifted up the stairs, the melody so very poignant.

'I forgot to tell you my brother has a wonderful voice.' Abigail squeezed her hand and they started down the steps.

This was her wedding march, sung by her groom. Truly, no orchestra would have sounded better.

All the dreaming is broken through,
Both what is done and undone I rue.
Nothing is steadfast, nothing is true
But your love for me and my love for you,
My dearest, dearest heart.

For all that the words did not fit their situation, they were beautiful and touching.

Peter, standing beside Isaiah, cast him a sidelong glance that clearly stated his opinion—singing a wedding march was an odd thing to do.

A woman who was probably the vicar's wife stifled a small gasp. Having attended countless weddings, she must think this irregular.

Well, Felicia thought it was a lovely gesture and she was the one being sung to.

When the winds are loud, when the winds are low,
When roses come, when roses go,
One thought, one feeling is all I know,
My dearest, dearest heart!

At least Miss Shirls dabbed her eyes, clearly touched by the tune and the tenderness in the singer's voice.

Isaiah began to sing the last verse, but stopped abruptly and thank goodness he did. She knew the song and at a point it became quite grim.

'Better to leave off with wind and roses,' he whispered, taking her hand from Abigail's and tucking her fingers into the crook of his arm. He tipped his head sideways, his breath skimming her hair. 'I'm sorry, I should have thought to make this better. "My dearest heart" was all I could come up with in the moment.'

The vicar opened his Bible, glanced back and forth between the bride and groom, then he nodded at Peter and Miss Shirls.

'Dearly beloved, we are gathered here in the sight of God to unite this man and this woman in holy matrimony...'

Yes, for better or for worse, here she stood, seconds from becoming Lady Scarsfeld.

If only her sisters were here, it would make this feel more like a proper wedding.

All of a sudden she felt utterly alone. She was becoming part of a family of people she did not even know and Peter was going back to London this afternoon.

She hung on tightly to Isaiah's arm to keep her fingers from trembling.

Of course he noticed. It must be why he covered her hand with his, giving it a bolstering squeeze. Had he smiled at her it would have put her at ease, but the corners of his mouth were pinched tight.

At least one person was smiling. Abigail grinned as

merrily as a ray of sunshine bursting through a bank of storm clouds.

Felicia had to imagine that her mother was smiling, too. Mama's dream was about to come true.

Felicia looked into her groom's eyes when the vicar prompted her to say, 'I do.'

But did she? Was her dream about to come true?

She had made the decision two or three times already, but now it was for ever. Once the vow was uttered, it could not be renounced. All vows were important, but this one was sacred. One's reasons for repeating them had no bearing on their significance.

Searching her groom's eyes, Felicia looked for reassurance that she was doing the right thing, that the gold ring about to circle her finger was where it ought to be.

What she saw startled her, caught her breath and tripped her heart all over itself.

Felicia? His mouth moved, but his voice did not come out.

'Are you afraid of me, Isaiah?' How could he possibly be? And yet there was no denying what she could see.

The minister looked at them both, brows arched and no doubt wondering what was quietly passing between them.

He nodded. 'This—*you*—is not what I expected.'

'You have changed your mind.' Her stomach gave a sickening heave.

As rejections went this was a humiliating one. More painful than she could have imagined. It made the shame of standing alone at a ball while watching every other lady dance seem trivial.

Pressing her hand to her middle, she prayed for the

strength to walk calmly from the room without creating a scene.

'I have not changed my mind. But I did not expect to care who it was that I married—and now I find that I do care. And that scares me. Please Felicia, do not go back to London.'

How could she not believe him? His expression in the moment was completely unguarded. 'Here I am, Isaiah, and here I will stay.'

The vicar cleared his throat. 'Let us carry on. Felicia Merry Penneyjons, do you take this man to be your lawfully wedded husband?'

Isaiah took both of her hands in his and gripped them tight.

'Yes, I do.' She held his gaze hard, making the vow with her eyes as well as her words. A tremor passed through his fingers. Somehow the sensation raced up her arms, lodged in her heart and left it trembling.

'Isaiah Elphalet Maxwell, Viscount Scarsfeld, do you take Felicia Merry Pennyjons to be your lawfully wedded wife?'

'I do.'

'You may place the ring on your bride's hand,' the vicar instructed.

Isaiah held her fingers, slowly slipping the warm gold over her knuckles and into place.

'I now pronounce you man and wife.' The vicar closed his Bible.

There, it was done.

Someone sniffled—the vicar's wife, she thought, but did not turn her gaze to look.

Her attention was all for her new husband.

And he had promised her a kiss. The expectation of it had left her half-breathless all morning. If what he had given her last night had been only a foretaste, what would his genuine kiss be like?

Indeed, she was intrigued to explore this aspect of her marriage to Isaiah. He had left the direction it would take up to her, after all, and, to be honest, the images popping into her mind were fascinating.

Glancing about, she saw everyone grinning in anticipation of the happy sealing of the vows.

'You may kiss your bride, my lord,' the vicar stated.

'You may kiss your bride, my lord,' the vicar repeated, as if Isaiah had somehow forgotten.

No man with blood in his veins should need reminding. Not with his wife's cheeks flushing pink in expectation, her green eyes sparkling in happy expectation.

He had promised her a kiss. One that was more than the breath he had grazed her mouth with last night.

But this morning, in the cold light of day, he had promised himself he would not kiss her. It was true what he had admitted about her frightening him. It was all too easy to imagine losing his heart to her.

Unbearable heartache lay that way. Just the thought of possibly suffering another such loss as he had with his mother terrified him.

Yet with everyone looking on, what was he to do? A kiss was expected.

At his obvious hesitation, Felicia's smile sagged.

Someone tugged on his arm.

Abigail?

She pulled him down to whisper in his ear, 'I made

her bouquet in your name, but you must do the kissing yourself.'

Of course he must—and yet he must not. The scents of a feast drifted in from the dining room. The wedding breakfast awaited.

The vicar frowned. Peter curled his fists. Miss Shirls shook her head, pursing her lips.

All right, then. With what he hoped was a smile, he placed his hands on Felicia's shoulders, drew her towards him.

He kissed her cheek.

A half-hearted cheer went up from those in the parlour. Also from a few of the servants who had gathered in doorways to watch the nuptials.

'Shall we go into the dining room, Lady Scarsfeld?'

His bride looked down at her hand, turned the gold band on her finger.

'I will freshen up and meet you in a few moments, Lord Scarsfeld.'

He deserved the distance she put between them by using his title. He only wondered if the kiss on her cheek had insulted her, or broken her heart.

While he watched her hurry out of the parlour, Miss Shirls marched up to him.

'That was not well done, my lord, especially if you intend to put an heir in the nursery.'

No doubt that was why the nanny assumed he had decided to marry, to get an heir. No one but Felicia knew the real reason for it.

But Miss Shirls was correct, the kiss had not been well done. Why had he not just given Felicia a formal peck on the lips?

Because he knew it would be impossible, was why not. He barely withheld a snort at the thought. There could never be a formal kiss between them, he feared.

There was something there—a draw, a small wavering flame that, once kindled, would ignite in a blaze. A blaze that would consume him.

He had been consumed once before when love had walked away. He would not risk being left in ashes again.

Which did not change the fact that he had to try to make up for what he had done—or not done as the case was.

'I will meet you in the dining room, Miss Shirls.'

He had no idea how to set this straight with Felicia, only that he must find her and try to.

Several moments later he found her in the conservatory, standing at the window gazing out, her back straight and her arms crossed over her middle.

'It has been pointed out that I have behaved badly towards you.'

She spun about, her hand at her throat.

'You startled me, my lord.'

'I beg your pardon.' He strode forward. What could he possibly say to set things right?

'Surely there is no need.' She smiled at him, but it was easy to see the hurt behind the gesture. 'If it was Peter, he is very protective and—'

'It was Miss Shirls—and Abigail. But more than that, my own conscience.'

'I don't know why you would—'

'Of course you do, Felicia. You are simply trying to make me feel better about how I mishandled our wedding. I ought to have listened to my sister and her governess when they said there ought to be pretty decorations and music.'

'Well, we did manage without them. And here we are, Lord and Lady Scarsfeld, none the less.'

'None the less—you ought to have fond memories of your wedding day. I am sorry you do not have them.'

'That is not quite true. Your song for me was beautiful. Not many brides are serenaded by their grooms for their wedding march.'

'Had I given it more thought, I would have come up with something more cheerful. I should have and I apologise—for all of it.'

'Will you sing the end of the song for me?'

'Are you certain?' It was rather morbid.

'I would like to hear it, so, yes, please, do sing it.'

Just because he had a decent voice did not mean he enjoyed singing. He would not have done it for the ceremony had he not blundered in neglecting to plan music for her wedding march.

He cleared his throat, gazed out at the frigid vista beyond the window.

The time is weary, the year is old,
And the light of the lily burns close to the mould:
The grave is cruel, the grave is cold,
But the other side is the city of gold,
My dearest heart!
My darling, darling, my darling heart.

'There, you see, once one gets past the grim time there is the city of gold.'

Yes, in the song there was, but—

She touched him, her fingers pressing lightly on his heart. The wedding band caught a wink of sunlight streaking in the window and glowed warmly on her finger.

'May I speak freely, Isaiah?'

'Of course, we have already established that there should be candour between us.'

There was something about the way she said his name that arrowed straight to his heart, but not in a way that made him feel vulnerable. No, it felt comfortable—familiar and strange all at once.

'I recognise that you fear me, although I cannot imagine why. I am not at all terrifying or judgemental. But one day I will know the reason because you will reveal it to me. I have confidence that you will come to trust me, Isaiah. Perhaps in time we will have our city of gold—just like the song says.'

She had far too much confidence in what he would reveal. He did not wish to even think about a past which had made him the bitter man he was today, let alone discuss it.

'I owe you something,' he said. 'I made you a promise and I did not keep it.'

She bit her bottom lip and, by it, silently told him that she knew he meant the kiss he had withheld.

Without a word, she spun about, started to walk away from him.

He caught her arm, halting her progress, but still she did not turn to look at him.

'Felicia?'

Placing his hands on her shoulders, he turned her to face him.

Still, she avoided his gaze and instead looked over his shoulder as if she found something fascinating happening on the lake. With one finger under her chin he turned her face until she could look nowhere but into his eyes.

'I will not be an obligation to be fulfilled,' she whispered, her eyes turning dark green with her frown. Firmly she removed his hand. 'Our guests are waiting. I will meet you in the dining room.'

In walking away, she brushed her cheek with the back of her hand. From behind he could not see her tears, but he felt them. They sliced his heart as if with a dull knife.

Felicia, an obligation?

She had been that in the beginning, when she had only been an idea—a solution to a problem.

But the woman walking away from him was not that. Somehow she had seen him, had looked past his surly nature and glimpsed a golden city.

She could not know, nor did he dare reveal, that the reason he had not kissed her was because it would be so much more than a gesture. By indulging in the pleasure, he risked losing his heart.

So here he stood, the worst sort of cad. What kind of man let his wife suffer a broken heart so that he would not risk one for himself?

A miserable one. One who was a failure only moments into the marriage.

Chapter Six

Felicia sat straight-backed in the middle of the Viscountess's wide bed, feeling rather small. That was odd, she had never felt small.

Back at home her toes dangled off the mattress when she stretched out.

Back at home she was never lonely, either. There had always been the company of her younger sister in their cosy bedroom. Ginny snored and it was annoying, but she would take being sleepless thanks to her sister's noise over this silence.

'Not that I should expect—or even want anything different. I did not expect to make a love match.'

Indeed, the fact that she had made a match at all ought to be comfort enough.

'And it would be enough had you not teased me with that breathy little kiss,' she said to the man who was probably blissfully sleeping in the chamber across the hall from hers.

Honestly, she had held no hope of anything but friendship.

If only he had not kissed her and left the taste of his breath lingering in her mind. To be fair, it was not all his fault. If she had not brought the subject up, he never would have done so.

She had never tasted a man before, nor even got close enough to know the intimate smell of one. She had hugged her father and Peter many times, but that hardly counted.

A golden city, indeed. What had got into her, pushing Isaiah that way? She knew he was wounded. She had even threatened to discover why.

If he wanted her to know, he would reveal why without her nosing about. If he did not, it was none of her business.

'Unless it really is my calling to bring you happiness.'

Then again, it was presumptuous of her to imagine so, was it not?

'But on the other hand you summoned me here, married me.'

A wife did have a certain obligation to her husband. Felicia had grown up watching her mother guide her father along life's path.

For her effort, Mama never went without a kiss.

One of the stories that Mama had been fond of telling her girls was that she had made a love match, although she had not realised it until after the wedding night. By the dawn of their first day of marriage her parents were deliriously smitten with each other.

Clearly Felicia was not going to share her mother's lot. Isaiah had told her the decision about intimacy in their marriage was up to her, but she suspected it was not completely true. The man had shied away from giving her the courtesy of a wedding kiss and was unlikely to welcome her to his bed.

Hmm. What was there keeping her from putting that assumption to the test? His chamber door was no more than fifteen steps from hers.

All right, then. She yanked the blankets off her legs and shot out of bed.

In the eyes of the law she had every right to enter his room.

If she found him soundly sleeping, blissfully unmoved by his virgin bride being only steps away, she would trouble him no more over the issue.

One could not force affection. Loving feelings might sprout and grow, but they could never be coerced.

Shrugging into her robe, she walked towards the door in long determined steps. Somewhat determined, that was. It seemed the closer she got to reaching for her door knob, the less sure she was of going through with this little test.

What if he was awake and invited her to share his bed?

Taking such a step was something she would prefer to wait for, would she not?

Tonight her intention was only to discover if he might be willing, one day in the future, to take it.

She reached for the knob, turned it. It was not unreasonable to want to know such a thing—what course her life would take.

With a bolstering breath, she stepped into the hallway.

'Good evening, Felicia,' a deep voice rumbled from beside her—close beside her.

Spinning sideways, she found Isaiah, his shoulder leaning against the wall only feet from her doorway, his arms crossed over his chest and one bare foot leisurely propped over the other.

'What are you doing in the hallway?' she asked. 'It is awfully late.'

'I was on my way back from the—the kitchen—I heard you talking. I was just reassuring myself that all was well.'

'Oh… I was talking in my sleep, that's all.' What was it she had muttered aloud? 'I hope I did not embarrass myself by saying something nonsensical.'

Please let it have sounded nonsensical!

What on earth had she revealed? And now here she was, caught out.

'What are you doing out so late?' he asked, straightening away from the wall.

'Looking for something.'

That wretched kiss he had failed to deliver, was what. Staring at him in the dim hallway, all sleepy-eyed and dishevelled, she had to admit it had been her purpose in going to his room all along.

For all she had told herself she wanted some sort of revelation as to what her future held, she knew it had not been the whole reason.

She wanted that kiss—she wanted it now.

In theory she wanted it now. In the privacy of her mind she was indulging in it. Standing in the dim hall, she imagined him with his— Never mind that.

In reality, she was far too nervous to act on what she wanted.

'What are you missing?'

She could hardly let it be an earring or a shoe or anything that would cause the staff hours of useless searching.

'Dessert. I woke up hungry and am going to the kitchen to have some.'

'I'll go with you.'

'But you just came from there. I'm certain I can find my way to the kitchen and back. Scarsfeld is my home now, after all.'

'I only thought since we are both awake, we might spend the time together.'

She could hardly tell him that the more time she spent with him, the more she wanted what he owed her.

One thing was certain—she would never drag a kiss from him. Either he would give it on his own or she would not have it.

'You ought to get back to sleep. I'm sure your duties as Viscount make a high demand on your time.'

'The truth is, I have not yet been to sleep.'

He hadn't? Well, it was good that she had made her discovery without having to invade his sanctuary.

'Come along, then,' she said as boldly as if this had been her home all along and he newly come to it.

'Perhaps we are over-weary from little sleep last night and a busy day today.'

'They say it happens. But may I be honest about why I cannot sleep?'

'You know you can be, Felicia.'

He might not feel the same if he knew all that was tumbling about in her mind. For instance, last night it appeared he had little on under his robe. He would be scandalised to know where her mind was freely wandering. Were she not now a married woman, Felicia would be scandalised, too.

'I'm awake because I am lonely.' She could reveal this much truth. 'The only person in the world who I have known for more than a few days has gone home to London. No one here really knows me, nor do I know them. There has not been a moment of my life where I was more than calling distance from someone who knows me inside out, as I know them.'

'All the more reason for us to spend this time together.'

'There really is no need to go all the way to the kitchen. The house is cold and my chamber is right here, already warm.'

He looked past her shoulder. It was hard to read his expression in the dim light of the hallway. She sensed, though, that he saw things in the room which she did not.

Ghosts of the past? Of course he would have them.

Good? Bad? Both, no doubt, since life tended to be a mixture of blessings and trials.

'Since you are hungry, we will go to the kitchen.' He took a few steps towards the stairs.

Watching his purposeful stride, she reminded herself to keep patience with his somewhat imperious manner. He was the Viscount, after all, and accustomed to having everyone jump to do his bidding.

With Felicia's mother as an example to go by, this was not going to be easy. Mama was Papa's equal, his best friend and confidante.

When it came to marriage, Felicia wanted nothing

less. Love match aside, she would not be under Lord
Scarsfeld's thumb.

But for now, she rushed to catch him up. They'd had
a pleasant time together last night and perhaps tonight
would be the same.

'Why can't you sleep, Isaiah?'

'To tell you the truth, Felicia, I fear the same thing
you do. Being lonely. Until Abigail came to me, I knew
nothing else. And now that she might be taken away—
I—' He shook his head as if the words were too painful to be uttered. 'What if our marriage is not enough
to dissuade Lord and Lady Penfield? It is possible that
they are determined to raise her in London and nothing I do will change their minds.'

'We will do our best to prevent that.'

Then, as if it were the most natural thing in the
world, he caught her hand and held it as they walked
towards the kitchen.

Coming into the welcoming space, breathing in the
lingering scents of cinnamon and cloves, she sat on one
of the chairs which Isaiah pulled up to the table in the
centre of the room.

She watched him—well, his back and the way his
muscles moved under the robe—while he prepared tea.

Brewing tea was not something a viscount typically
knew how to do. She did admire him for not being above
the task. Perhaps it was a result of the hours he had spent
here with the cook when he was young.

'I wonder,' he murmured, his shoulders going suddenly still, 'if we are not as alone as we each feel at
the moment.'

He must be right about that since she had not felt the

sting of missing her family since Isaiah had taken her hand while escorting her to the kitchen.

'We do have each other in this—after all, we are allies united in our cause,' she said.

He carried two steaming cups to table, then sat on the chair beside her, not across as he had last night.

He lifted his cup as if to give a toast. She raised hers and china clinked.

'To our success, Felicia.'

And then he smiled. Truly and naturally smiled.

It was all she could do not to slip off the chair. She had waited, hoping to see this gesture, and it left her quite undone.

Also, he was fairly easy for her to read. The success he referred to was about the situation regarding Abigail—but not completely that.

Subtly, he was also referring to them—to their brand-new marriage.

No doubt he was trying to hide the thought from her, but how could he?

Wives knew things…even those new to the position did.

'To our success,' she answered, quite certain he was not aware of the way her heart flipped and fluttered.

Isaiah huddled into his coat while he walked towards the stable. Head down against the chill, he made his way briskly along the path leading from the manor, across a bridge and then a meadow to the large stone barn.

He needed to speak with the stableman. This time of year one could not be certain of when a heavy storm might occur. It would be wise to find what was needed, then make a trip to the village and lay in supplies, feed for the animals and food for people who lived at Scarsfeld.

Christmas gifts for Abigail, too. While he would not cut a Christmas tree and decorate it, he would provide the Yule log. There would be a large stack of presents set in front of the fireplace for his sister to open on Christmas morning.

After his meeting with the stableman, he would visit Mrs Muldoon in the kitchen. This afternoon he would take the carriage to Windermere and purchase all they needed.

Some gentlemen would distain the chore but Isaiah wanted to make sure nothing was forgotten. Glancing back at the house, he spotted Abigail coming out of the conservatory followed closely by Felicia.

They appeared to be racing each other down the steps. The tinkle of laughter reached him across the distance.

He inhaled, intending to shout for them to go back inside, those steps were slippery. Before he could open his mouth, they were safely down and beginning a snowball fight.

Had he not needed to meet with the stableman, he might have joined in. Snowball fights were one of the things he and his sister enjoyed doing together.

As far as he was concerned, it was the one bright part of winter weather. That and remaining sensibly inside near a warm fire.

And soup. He greatly enjoyed the soups and stews Mrs Muldoon prepared in the cold weather.

What did Felicia enjoy? he wondered while entering the stable and relishing the warmth and the scent of wood smouldering in the stove. Whatever it was, he would do his best to indulge her in it.

He owed her more than he could ever repay.

But, no, even though he did, that was not the reason he wanted to make her happy.

Truthfully, it was because he enjoyed her company, found her easy smiles engaging.

Last night they had spent an hour over tea while she told him about her childhood. She shared the story of her parents' shocking deaths and how Peter had suddenly become Viscount, how being only a few years older than Felicia's older sister, he had stepped into the role of guardian and pulled them all through it.

During a lighter part of the conversation, she revealed how she and her sisters enjoyed shopping. The three of them had a merry time purchasing hats and gowns, but more than that they enjoyed getting secret gifts for each other.

Since she took so much joy in shopping—an activity that he avoided when he could—he wondered if Felicia would like to accompany him to Windermere. She would be a big help when it came to picking out gifts for Abigail and the children of the staff, along with all the others living at Scarsfeld.

If she did come along, it would make it a pleasure instead of a chore.

'Good day, my lord.' The stableman, Mr Reeves, popped his head up from behind a stall gate. 'A storm's coming in, I feel it down in my bones.'

'Do they tell you when—your bones?'

'The closer it gets the more they ache, so in a way they do.'

'I'm going to Windermere for supplies. If there is to be a storm, we should buy extra goods.'

'I'll write a list and bring it up to the house.' Mr Reeves gave him a wrinkled smile. 'And congratulations on your marriage, sir. My wife tells me Lady Scarsfeld is a well-needed ray of light in the manor house. Ah, but I've let my tongue run amok again. Hilde will call me to task if she finds out.'

'She will not hear it from me, Mr Reeves. And you need not bother making a trip to the house. I'll come by for the list on my way out—in a couple of hours, I think.'

'I will see you then.'

Once back in the open air, he huddled deeper into his coat. The temperature was dropping quickly. Even though there was only a scattering of clouds in the bright blue sky, the sooner he made his trip to Windermere and returned, the better. Mr Reeves's bones were well known to be a reliable predictor of foul weather.

For all that Isaiah disliked inclement weather, he wondered if it might serve a purpose.

A blizzard would prevent train travel. Travel by coach would be even more unlikely.

With any luck Abigail's aunt and uncle would be delayed—for ever.

The thought was uncharitable, of course. Abigail should get to know her family. They might be good-hearted people. But given what their intentions were, he could not find it in his heart to wish them welcome.

He well remembered how it felt to be ripped away

from home and he would not have that happen to his little sister. She was his to protect, his to nurture and love.

Now that Felicia was here Lord and Lady Penfield could not claim she lacked a woman's guidance.

It was clear to see, just in this short time, how well Abigail was taking to Felicia.

At first, it had taken him aback, seeing them together, laughing and talking about frills, books and the things girls loved.

All these years he'd assumed he was enough for Abigail, that the love he gave her was all she needed. Sending for Felicia had been for show, for an additional defence in keeping his sister where she belonged.

For as wrong as he had been in thinking Felicia could live here more a guest than a wife, he had also been that wrong about Abigail's needs.

Seeing the way she was with Felicia, so genuinely happy to be with her—to have a sister of her own—his first, and selfish, emotion had been a brief but sharp stab of jealousy.

Since that stormy night when his sister had been delivered to him, he thought he had been all Abigail needed. What a shock it was to discover he was wrong in believing so.

More of a shock was how quickly his jealousy changed to gratitude. He was more than lucky to have wed the lady he had.

How things had changed from a week ago when his only requirement of a bride was that she be willing.

This afternoon he found himself looking for reasons to be in Felicia's company.

The trip to the village and then the shopping would take a few hours. After that he would take her to dinner.

Funny, he could not recall an afternoon he had looked forward to more than this one.

Felicia balanced three dolls in the crook of her arm while pointing to four more she wanted.

No one would be aware that her toes were tapping under her skirt but they were, propelled by 'Deck the Halls' and 'Jingle Bells,' which rang merrily in her mind.

Lady Scarsfeld had a purpose! Isaiah, having requested her help in purchasing a toy for each of the estate children, had given her one that suited very well.

She was skilled at shopping and apparently there was no budget to be held accountable to. Had funds been an issue surely he would have mentioned it?

Setting the dolls on the counter, she turned her attention to sailing boats.

'Lord Scarsfeld is being especially generous this Christmas,' the proprietress of the shop commented with a great grin.

Felicia would know the truth of it when her husband returned from purchasing supplies for the stable.

While he had told her to buy whatever she needed, not all opinions were equal when it came to Christmas gift giving.

For instance, that one sweet-looking doll remaining on the shelf had eyes the most beautiful shade of brown and hair the colour of wheat. It would not be in the spirit of Christmas to leave it to gather dust when a child might be enjoying it.

Now that Felicia was Lady Scarsfeld some decisions were for her to make.

After she set a dozen sailing boats on the counter with the dolls, she went in search of balls, drums and books.

By the time Isaiah returned from taking care of his business, the counter would be buried under games, hats, scarves and whatever else she could think of which might make a child dance in delight on Christmas morning. Seeing the children happy would certainly make Felicia dance in delight.

The bell on the door jingled, announcing someone had come inside.

'Felicia?'

The moment of reckoning was upon her. She turned towards the door, her smile firmly in place.

Isaiah did look stunned, but to his credit recovered quickly.

'Abigail will be busy all year playing with all of—' he indicated the toys piled on the counter with a wave of his hand '—this. It was kind of you to go to the trouble.'

'Oh, indeed! But these are for the other children. Abigail's gifts are behind the counter.'

'Ought I to hire an extra carriage to cart all this home?'

Rather, yes. 'We have yet to visit the hat shop, so perhaps it would be wise.'

No doubt her husband was not used to shopping with a woman, especially at this most wonderful time of the year.

'And I imagine we will not leave Windermere without a trip to the sweet shop?' he asked. His dark brows slashed downwards, giving him a severe expression.

The woman behind the counter shuffled back a step, no doubt quaking at his brooding look.

What Felicia saw was something different. He was teasing rather than testy. Truly, the sparkle in those brown depths was clear to see if one cared to look closely enough. Because she did, it was all she could do not to hug him. Had the shopkeeper not been staring, open-mouthed, Felicia would have.

'I adore sweets. Thank you for suggesting it.'

He opened the shop door, standing to one side to let her pass. As she did, he caught her elbow.

'I would wager that you have never spent one dull Christmas in your life,' he whispered close to her ear.

'A wager you would win. And I do not intend for this to be the first, Isaiah.'

What was that? Yes, just there the corner of his mouth tipped—or quirked.

Not a smile, quite, but far from a scowl.

How would he react when she began to deck his halls tomorrow?

Chapter Seven

As it turned out, the stableman's bones proved to be correct again.

Wind howled through the streets of Windermere so ferociously that those sitting near the windows in the hotel lobby moved to the centre of the room.

'I am sorry, Lord Scarsfeld, but there is only one room available. So many people seeking shelter from the windstorm. Why, one gentleman has even rented the sofa in front of the fireplace.'

This would not do. It was one thing to spend quiet moments alone in the Scarsfeld kitchen with Felicia, but here at the hotel with one room having one bed—it would not suit.

'I will hire the chair beside the sofa,' he insisted.

'A private word, my lord?' Felicia tugged him away from the counter and led him a few steps beyond the clerk's hearing.

'You must share the room with me, Isaiah.'

Certainly not! He had promised her a choice. He would not have one foisted upon her by sharing her room and then finding himself unable to keep his hands to himself.

He might appear to be as emotionally distant as a stone, but something was changing inside him and it was happening too quickly for his peace of mind.

'If the chair does not suit, I will stretch out on the floor.'

'I would not advise it. What will people think? Newlywed and sleeping apart? If you intend to convince Lord and Lady Penfield that Abigail is better off with us, we must appear to be a contented, devoted family.'

'We shall begin when they arrive.'

She held his hand, smiled, then kissed his cheek. 'Perhaps you have not noticed everyone has been looking at us. If you do not go upstairs with me they will begin to talk. You know very well how easily gossip gets about. What is to say that Abigail's aunt and uncle will not hear of our coldness to each other?'

She was correct. Gossip did have a life of its own. His sudden marriage was bound to be a source of speculation as it was.

Keeping hold of her hand, he walked back to the desk.

'The room will do nicely.'

The receptionist did not ask if they had baggage to be brought up. No doubt he assumed that, like so many others, they were in town for the day and had become stranded by the weather.

Going up the stairs, Felicia's hand clutching his arm and having possession of a key to a room, he realised how very fortunate he was.

Had the wind risen an hour later they would have

been caught out in it. They, the drivers and the poor beasts pulling the carriage would have been in peril.

It was no less than a tempest outside. Windows rattled in their frames, even paintings on the stairwell wall seemed to be vibrating.

'Here we are,' he said. Stopping in front of room six, he turned the key in the lock. 'I've spent the night in this room on occasion. It is comfortable.'

But cold. The fire had not yet been lit. And no wonder, the staff being so busy with people seeking shelter.

Felicia went in ahead of him. He closed the door, then knelt in front the hearth to build the fire.

Glancing over his shoulder, he watched her stroll about the room while removing her hat. She patted the bed as if testing it for softness. He wondered if she liked a mattress soft, or firm the way he did.

Flames ignited quickly in the tinder, but it might take time for the logs to catch fire.

He stood up, wiping his hands on his trousers.

'Shall I ask the kitchen to send something up? Dessert, perhaps, tea or coffee?'

'Tarts would be delightful—and a pot of good hot tea.'

He removed his coat, then placed it across the back of one of the two chairs in the room.

'Thank you for that, down in the lobby.' He rubbed his hands in front of the growing flames. 'I had not thought of presenting an image.'

After slipping off her coat and folding it neatly, Felicia set it on the other chair. Coming to stand beside him, she turned her palms towards the growing flames.

'I hope you do not take it amiss if I act overly familiar when the Penfields are present. The last thing I would wish is for my actions to offend you.'

'Probably not the last thing. The last would be having to say goodbye to Abigail.'

She was correct, yet at the same time he did not wish to offend Felicia, to have her think he was taking liberties.

Truth to tell, the thought of taking liberties in the guise of presenting a loving marriage to the Penfields had crossed his mind. Not just crossed, but lingered and presented images which a man set on keeping his heart to himself ought not to have.

'In the spirit of our cause, I will not take anything you do amiss.' She turned her hands to warm the backs. 'Besides, I like you. It should not be so difficult to portray feelings of friendship.'

An odd sensation buzzed in his belly. He was not used to having friends. Acquaintances who did not make demands of his heart, he had some of those, but the friendship Felicia spoke of was something else.

What her eyes told him was that what she had so casually called friendship might mean something more.

Surely she did not realise what her expression revealed.

A quiet rap sounded on the door.

'You may enter,' he announced.

A young maid, still a child really, stepped into the room.

'I've brought a pitcher of clean water and towels, Lord Scarsfeld.' She set them beside the washstand. 'My brother, Michael, is coming behind me bringing more wood for the fire. Shall I have a bath sent up, my lady?'

A what? In here? No, there was not a bit of privacy for such a thing. He would never survive watching Felicia bathe. Even though she was his wife and it would not be a sin—it felt very much as though it was.

'Please do not go to the trouble. I'm certain you have more to do than you can manage already,' Felicia answered.

Thank you, God.

Isaiah gave the girl a coin in thanks for offering to deliver the order for tarts and tea.

'Oh, one moment, miss!' Felicia opened her purse and plucked out two peppermint sticks. She gave one to the girl, then one to the boy who had had just finished stacking the wood beside the hearth. 'Have a very happy Christmas season.'

'Thank you, Lady Scarsfeld!' the children said as one.

They went out the door, their smiles shining as bright as the full moon coming into view through the window as it rose over the hills. The huge, bright orb cast shadows on the bed from a nearby tree. The spindly etchings lashed madly on the flowered quilt.

With the door shut and the two of them standing inches apart in front of the hearth, the room felt intensely intimate.

The bed in the room, to be precise.

In his mind it throbbed like a heartbeat.

Fondness for his wife was growing in a way he had not anticipated. She neatly threatened the iron safe in which he kept his heart safely stowed. Every time she smiled, each time she laughed, she spun the rusty lock.

It was as if she knew the combination and was clicking the numbers in place one by one.

He feared that one day, without warning, the heavy iron door would squeal open and he would once again be left vulnerable.

Judging by the blush on her cheeks, she felt the pulsing bed in the same way he did.

'You are blushing, Isaiah.'

Curse it!

'No more than you are.'

Which was acceptable for a woman, but certainly not for a viscount who tried to portray himself as a man of cool emotions.

'It is rather funny, don't you think?' she asked.

'It would do my image irreparable harm if anyone were to discover my weakness.'

'I will not divulge it, but honestly, expressing one's emotions is a strength rather than a weakness.'

'Not for everyone.' Not for him.

'If you mean—'

A knock on the door cut her off and not a moment too soon. The last thing he wanted to hear was that she felt his stony demeanour could be redeemed. He did not want it to be redeemed. It was safe in the dark where no one could really see him.

A woman carrying a tray laden with teapot, cups and two tarts entered the room.

'Good evening, Lord Scarsfeld,' she said soberly. Then, smiling at Felicia, she added, 'Lady Scarsfeld, it was kind of you to give my children sweets. Your generosity is all they can speak of.'

'Peppermint and children are a natural combination,' Felicia answered. 'How many more children are here?'

'Four, my lady.'

Felicia cast him a glance that the cook would not see. Offer peppermint sticks to the others, it clearly said—demanded.

His bride could have made the offer herself, but was giving him the chance to appear congenial.

He walked to the wretched beating bed and withdrew four peppermint sticks from Felicia's stash.

'With your permission, of course,' he said to the cook.

'That is very kind of you, sir.' The woman looked at him as if she was surprised to find that he was.

No more surprised than he was since it was really Felicia who was the kind one.

The cook went out of the room, leaving behind a pair of exceedingly delicious-smelling pastries. Fragrant steam rose from the teapot. Simply breathing it in made the room feel warmer.

'You will make me out a saint,' he said while pouring a cup of tea.

He blurted the first thing to come to his mind because he did not wish to return to the conversation from before the cook knocked on the door.

It would not do for Felicia to continue probing his heart.

Sitting across from each other in the red, overstuffed chairs, they drank the tea and ate the tarts, mostly in silence. Their only comments had to do with the weather, which continued to grow worse for all that the moon continued to shine through the window and on to the blasted bed.

Isaiah could not recall ever having been more irritated with a piece of innocent furniture.

No doubt it was because his thoughts about that particular piece were not at all innocent. Not wicked, either, since he was married to the lady plucking a stray pie crumb from her bodice, then popping it into her mouth.

Anything he did to her would be—

He stood up. 'I'll go downstairs to the taproom and give you time to prepare for bed. You need not stay awake. I might be quite late.'

'As you wish, my lord.'

My lord? He had not known her long, but long enough to understand that in addressing him as such, she meant quite the opposite of what she said.

Surely she did not mean she wished for him to stay while she prepared for bed—or that he should join her in it? But if not, what was it that she did mean?

Dash it! He was taking his confusion and going down—

Glass exploded into the room.

Felicia shrieked and leapt from the chair.

Glittering in the moonlight, razor-like splinters of the window blew in on the wind, scattering them throughout the room. He caught Felicia up, wrapped his arms around her and spun her away from the shards.

'What was that?' she gasped, her breath warm where she buried her face against his neck.

'A tree went down. It broke the window. Look, there is a limb on the bed.'

Over the rush of wind blowing inside, he heard

shouts of alarm coming from the rooms beside this one. Footsteps pounded on the stairs, some going up and some going down.

From what he could make of the shouts, the lobby windows had fared no better than this one had.

'Shall we go and spend the night downstairs?' She burrowed into him, seeking warmth.

'We are better off here. The fire is still going and we won't have to share it with a dozen other people.'

'The bed is unusable.'

'I have a plan.' He snatched his coat from the chair, shook it, then set it across her shoulders, giving it a tug under her chin. 'Here, Felicia, sit by the fire.'

She settled on the rug cross-legged while looking up at him. 'What are you going to do?'

'Make a tent. Will you be all right while I get it done?'

She nodded, but he could see that she was beginning to shiver with the icy air rushing inside.

As quickly as he could, he shook broken glass from the quilt and blankets. After that he dragged the chairs close to the fire and set them side by side. Draping the quilt over the chairs, he formed the back of the shelter.

Still he needed something to hold the blanket on the sides of the small tent to keep out the wind. And then something else to secure a blanket from the hearth mantel to form a roof that would funnel heat directly at them.

Ah, the curtain rod would work to anchor the blanket to the hearth if he wrapped and twisted it just so. The hall tree would hold up one wall of the shelter walls so he dragged it over.

Since the curtains were serving no purpose at the moment he placed them on top of the blankets.

What else? There was a large painting on the wall which would have to do to support the other make-shift wall.

In all he was satisfied with the tiny sanctuary, but one thing was needed. Protection from the cold floor.

He dragged the mattress off the frame and shoved it into the shelter. Then, after giving the pillows a good shake, he brought them over.

In all it took no more than ten minutes to build and would, in the end, be better than joining the grumbling, shivering people who would be gathering in the lobby.

'Why, Isaiah, I had no idea you had such a talent for construction.'

He settled shoulder to shoulder with her because there was room to do nothing else.

What he did not have to do was slip one arm around her shoulder and draw her against his side.

That action was required in the cause of shared warmth. Any man who allowed his wife to shiver when he could prevent it was not worthy of the name husband. He already felt unworthy of the title as it was.

'This is wonderful.' He knew she meant it because he thought she did not say things she did not mean. 'It's really warm and lovely in here. I nearly feel guilty being so cosy when other wives are not. I doubt all men have your talent for survival.'

'They would have, when they were young. It's what boys do, make tents and forts and the like.'

What the other wives would have was heat from their

husband's bodies to keep them comfortable—more than simply an arm about the shoulder.

'It might be a long time before the wind stops and we can go home. What shall we do to pass the time?'

'You choose.' As long as it did not involve reclining on the mattress he would go along with it.

'All right, then. There is no going back on my choice.' Her smile looked rather satisfied so he wondered what he was in for. 'I choose that we sing.'

'Sing?' It could have been worse, he supposed. There were many popular tunes they could entertain themselves with.

'Yes, Christmas carols.'

'I don't know many.' And the ones he did know he didn't care for.

'Never fear, I know them all.' She tapped her lip with one finger. Surely she had no idea what that gesture was doing to him. Then again, she might since he was probably blushing like a fresh-faced boy.

'It won't be "I Saw Three Ships." Peter says I sound like screeching cats when I sing it.'

'Surely not!'

She shrugged, squinting her lovely green eyes.

'You will see. Let's sing "Silent Night." I'm sure you must know that one.'

He knew it, of course—had stopped singing it years ago. This carol had been one that his mother would sing to him on Christmas Eve when she tucked him into bed. During the innocent times, her sweet voice sent him gently off to sleep. Since it was difficult to remember the sweet time without the bitter, he no longer sang it.

Felicia was looking at him...into him as if she read

the old heartache. 'But I think a longer one might be better. "The Twelve Days of Christmas"!'

'Have mercy,' he muttered.

'It is what I choose and we have a long night ahead of us.'

'"On the first day of Christmas, my true love gave to me a partridge in a pear tree…" Isaiah, you must sing along. We agreed on it.'

'"On the second day of Christmas…"' he sang along, thinking that Peter was correct about the quality of her voice. However, he could listen to it for hours if only to watch her face. She was aptly named Felicia Merry. He could not ever recall seeing a person take so much joy in an activity. Especially in one they did not excel at. '"My true love sent to me, two turtle doves and a partridge in a pear tree…"'

On the third day, the busy fellow added three French hens and, on the fourth, four calling birds.

'"On the fifth day of Christmas my true love sent to me, five g-o-o-l-d *r-i-i-ings*!"' Felicia drew this part out while wagging her hand and displaying her wedding band.

He went on singing, pretending he was unaware of the fact that he sat upon a mattress with his lawfully wedded wife.

Eight maids were now a-milking. His fingers twitched.

Ten lords were a-leaping and he wanted to leap… to take a risk.

When the twelve drummers were drumming, so was his heart…

The song was finished and so was he.

Out of breath, he whispered, 'Felicia.'

He touched her cheek with the backs of his fingers, felt her cheeks plump with her smile. Her skin was warm—softer than anything he had ever touched.

'I always keep my word, pay my debts.' Shifting his finger to her chin, he stroked the curve where there was the nearly imperceptible curve of a dimple.

He moved, closing the distance between their lips. She blocked his way with her fingertips. But then she pressed them to his mouth, her touch tender as they traced the curve of his bottom lip.

'I do not wish to be your debt.' She was not smiling. Her eyes held him—her captive—who could do nothing but surrender. 'I wish to be your wife.'

He kissed her fingers, then lowered them.

'You could never be a debt—not to any man, especially not to me.'

'There is the matter of sealing our vows with a kiss. That remains undone. So if you did mean them—'

'I did.'

And so he kissed her. Tenderly, respectfully, as befitted their friendship. But then she stopped, pulled away from the kiss, but still so close he felt the heat of her mouth puffing on his.

'Isaiah,' she breathed against his lips.

Then she kissed him. Heat swallowed him, sparks ignited in a kiss befitting of a marriage bed.

Which they were sitting upon.

One tumble backwards and—no, he did not dare.

Felicia ended the kiss, blinked wide and smiled.

'I've never been kissed before.' She was silent for a moment, leaving him to wonder if she had enjoyed it or had been horrified at how the match had been put to the flame searing them both. 'It was more wonderful than I imagined it would be.'

Her assessment of the kiss gratified him—rather a lot.

'I have been kissed, Felicia.' He stroked a lock of red hair which grazed the curve of her smile. 'And this was by far more wonderful than any of them.'

And exactly what did that mean? What course would their lives take from now on?

Since he could not take what he truly wanted of her and not keep his heart in the vault, he said, 'Lie down, Felicia, get some sleep. I'll keep the fire tended.'

Nodding she muttered, 'Tomorrow will be a busy day, I'm sure.'

She eased back on the mattress, gave him a small smile, then turned on her side, tucking the fingers of both hands under her cheek.

It looked rather as though she was praying.

While she drifted off into a dream, was she wondering the same thing he was?

What fire, exactly, would he be tending?

Chapter Eight

A woman kissed for the first time, especially at her ripe age, could hardly walk about the house in a romantic trance all day long.

For all that it felt lovely to be dancing on clouds, Felicia thought that she must find something productive to occupy her mind. After all, it was not as though her groom had given her a declaration of true, undying love.

No, and she would not have wished him to. Not yet—but at some point she thought she might wish it.

The kiss last night, for all that it had left her hot and breathless, had been no more than a road sign pointing the way. All she could do was follow the direction it indicated and see where it led to. Along the way she needed something to do.

Standing in the centre of the parlour, gazing around her, she knew what it was.

As luck would have it, Abigail came skipping into the room at that very moment, hugging her cat to her chest.

'Good morning, Sister,' Felicia greeted.

'And to you, Sister!' The child set the cat on the floor.

'You have other sisters, but you are my first and there are things I do not know.'

'Things such as?'

'Is it proper to greet you with a hug?'

'Very proper if it is what you wish to do.'

With a hop, Abigail leapt for her, wrapped her slender arms about Felicia's waist and held on tight.

'What do you think?' Felicia asked. 'Does this room need a Christmas tree?'

'Desperately. I've always thought the garlands and bows we put up seem rather sad without a tree.' Abigail twirled out of the hug. 'I've never had a tree.'

'Never?' This would not do!

'I told my brother it is rude to ask Father Christmas to come to a home without one.'

'How did he answer your valid point?'

'He didn't. He asked if I would rather live somewhere else, which I would not.'

If it was in Felicia's power to prevent such a horrible thing, she would.

'Let's go and find your brother and have him take us out to cut down a tree.' The wind was no longer blowing. It had stopped some time in the night while she was asleep. 'The sun is shining and it will be a grand adventure.'

'Isaiah is out for the day. He and the estate manager have gone out to see what damage the winds caused. It might be late by the time he gets home.'

'No matter. I only thought he might enjoy our outing.'

'We will still do it? Even without him?'

'Of course—just because we are girls does not mean

we cannot cut a Christmas tree. All we need is a saw and a sledge.'

'What a grand adventure! I'll get my coat.' Abigail ran, but stopped every ten steps to lift her arms and spin happily. 'Father Christmas is going to be so pleased to finally feel welcome this year!'

Within half an hour the two of them were bundled and pulling the sledge towards the woodlands. Not to be left behind, the cat rode along, sitting on the cover they would use for sliding the tree on to the sledge.

'There are so many to choose from,' Abigail said. 'How do we know which one is right?'

'We look for perfection in size and shape, then see if the tree tugs on our heartstrings.'

'I believe all of them are tugging on my heartstrings. Have you cut down many trees, Felicia?'

'This will be my first. In London we purchased them from Christmas tree sellers. All we ever needed do was to choose one and carry it home—well, we girls did the choosing. Peter and a strong lad from the tree lot carried it home. I imagine the process will be much the same out here, but the tree will be so much fresher.'

Entering a copse of cedar and spruce, they walked among the trees, pausing at each one to evaluate it.

Abigail asked a question of each of them. 'Are you my very first Christmas tree?' Then she waited quietly to see if it would answer.

Most did not, some whispered perhaps. But finally one stood out among the rest, very clearly giving the feeling that it was their tree. That it longed for nothing more in life than to be decorated, carolled around and to have Father Christmas admire it.

Felicia picked up the saw. She hoped she had the skill to fell a nine-foot tree. But how difficult could the back-and-forth motion really be?

She nearly wished the tree that called them had not been quite so tall, but only nearly. This one would look grand and lofty in the parlour.

It took a long time to finally cut it through the trunk, but when it fell they both danced about in the snow, cheering their accomplishment.

'We had better get this home.' Felicia glanced at the sky. Clouds were beginning to streak across it. They were only thin and wispy, but could change from fluffy to threatening in an instant.

The last thing Felicia wanted was for them to get caught out by the elements.

'Where are you, cat?' Abigail called. 'I didn't see her wander off, did you?'

'She was sitting on the sledge a moment ago.'

'Eloise!' Her little sister glanced about, her small hands on her waist. 'I should have made her stay home no matter how she batted at my skirt and meowed.'

'She is close by, I'm certain of it. Let's look for tracks.'

'Here are some, they go this way and then that and then—'

Abigail shrieked. A pair of red squirrels chattered.

A very large hawk swooped down from the sky, its target one unaware cat leaping playfully after leaves.

Abigail ran, waving her arms and shouting. Felicia

picked up the saw, waving it about in hopes that a gleam of sunshine on metal would dissuade the bird of prey from its intended meal.

All at once, Abigail took a tumble into the snow. She yelped.

Felicia reached the cat before the bird did. It flapped its beautiful wings and, with a high-pitched cry, flew away.

Snatching up Eloise, she carried her back to where Abigail sat, hip deep in snow.

'What a bad girl you are, Eloise!' Abigail clutched her pet close to her heart while admonishing her.

'We had best be on our way,' Felicia reached a hand down to Abigail. 'The weather looks as though it might take a nasty turn sooner rather than later.'

'I think I may have twisted my ankle.'

'Is it terribly painful?'

'Not wickedly terrible, only mildly terrible.'

Luckily this was not the first time Felicia had been required to help a sister with an injured ankle.

'Here, then.' Felicia helped Abigail to stand. 'You hold on to your kitty and I will carry you to the sledge. There is a space between the branches where you should fit nicely.'

With the cat safe from the hawk and her little sister secure on the sledge, and all the while clouds growing ever darker on the horizon, Felicia was more than a little anxious to reach home.

Luckily it was not far. Coming out of the copse of trees she could see Scarsfeld Manor in the distance. She could not help but smile at the pretty mansion. Funny how only looking at it gave her a sense of warmth, of belonging.

Having lived her whole life at Cliverton, she did miss home very much. But she also found that she was beginning to feel at home here.

Perhaps it was because she sensed Scarsfeld was where she was meant to be—in this place and with these people. It was a comforting thought.

'My brother will not take it well that I have been injured.'

'Surely he will understand this was simply an accident.'

'He won't. Isaiah hovers over me, thinking every minute I will land in some sort of trouble.'

'He is your brother, after all. Even male cousins act that way.'

'I imagine so, but Isaiah is worse than most. You know that our mother sent me to him when I was a squalling infant—wailing and squalling is how he describes me in the moment he first took me from the lawyer.'

'Yes, I did know that. I'm very sorry that you lost your mother when you were so very young.'

'I did not know anything about that at the time, but then later I did feel the loss of having a mother. It is why Isaiah told me he married in such a hurry. So I would have a sister to help me grow rather than be sent off to a school for young ladies.'

That was not why, but Abigail would never hear the truth of it from Felicia's lips.

'I would not have gone, of course. I would run away

before I did that.' Felicia glanced back at Abigail while she tugged the sledge. The child meant it.

'Well, here I am and you will not be going anywhere unless you wish to. But tell me, why will your brother be so distressed about your ankle? As far as injuries go it is a minor one. My sister, Ginny, sprained her ankle doing a pirouette in a pile of autumn leaves and was off her feet no more than a week.'

'He worries because of what happened when I was little. I do not recall the event, but Isaiah tells me that once I toddled out of the house smack into a snowstorm and no one noticed. He went into a rage at my nurse—not Miss Shirls, she was on holiday at the time—for her negligence and tore out of the house, thinking to find me dead. Of course I was not, but I was sitting beside the lake, half-frozen through.'

'Your poor brother must have felt awful about it.'

'He let the nurse go on the spot without a recommendation. When Miss Shirls returned from holiday she was even more outraged than Isaiah was.'

'It is understandable, is it not?'

'I suppose so, but, as protective as he is, I fear he will not take the results of our adventure well.'

'We will simply have to make this the most beautiful Christmas tree Father Christmas has ever seen. That should take the edge off his temper.'

'It should.' Even without looking back at Abigail, she knew her little sister did not believe it.

It was moments before sunset when Isaiah finally walked in the back door of Scarsfeld.

He needed a bath, then a warm drink splashed with

whisky while he sat in a plush chair in front of the fireplace.

The storm that Mr Reeves had predicted was getting closer and, according to him, it would be more wicked than he first felt it would be.

Given that it was only the stableman's bones saying so, perhaps it would not be really be apocalyptic in nature.

Walking towards the kitchen and the delicious smells wafting out of it, he paused and heard—singing.

Felicia's merry voice, along with Abigail's and Miss Shirls's, drifted out of the open parlour doors.

Standing in the hallway, he listened. While not in perfect harmony, there seemed to be a great deal of joy in the singing.

Perhaps Christmas carols were not so heartbreaking after all. If he could only get himself to live in the present as he ought to and not the past, he might even enjoy them.

What better time than now to attempt to adopt a more cheerful spirit?

Choosing levity over a bath, drink and cosy chair, he continued down the hallway.

He smelled it before he saw it.

It could not be—and yet—his chest ached with the need to breathe, his hands grew damp.

His reaction to a Christmas tree was extreme, he understood that. Yet there he stood, thrown back into the past, and there wasn't a thing he could do to prevent the tumble.

Memories assailed him before he ever set eyes on the blasted tree. Years fell away and, standing in the hallway, he did not hear happy voices in the parlour, but rather a rage of thunder—an echo of a blizzard crashing against the walls of Scarsfeld.

At first he had welcomed the storm because Mother would not end her visit tomorrow afternoon as she planned to. They would be mother and son, sharing the jolly times they used to before she married Lord Penfield.

For this one happy Christmas they would be as they had been before her marriage. Just him and Mama, loving each other so very deeply. No one would be more important to Mama today than he would be.

It was Christmas! He had decorated the tree, as far up as he could reach, with the special ornaments he and Mama always used. Each one had a story, each one cherished. In the morning, while he unwrapped the gifts that Father Christmas would leave under the tree, she would tell him stories about his father. He knew from her that Papa had been wonderful, loving and the best man a son could ever hope to be descended from. He had always felt an ache listening to his mother's stories because, as wonderful as her recollections were, he had been a baby when Papa died and had no memories of his own.

But he did have memories of his stepfather, ones he wished he did not have.

But here it was, Christmas—everything should be right, but it was not. Even though Mama had come to visit without her husband, something felt wrong, wrong with Mama.

But he was only a child and trusted that Father Christmas, when he came, would make it all right. In the morning, good things would happen and he would no longer remember the way his mother had looked at him so oddly last night.

No doubt she had a stomach ache or something of the sort and that was why she did not sing him to sleep with 'Silent Night.' Or she probably had a headache and that was why she stood in his bedroom doorway, sober faced and making him feel that she did not know who he was.

It seemed to take a long time to fall asleep because Mama did not sing him the song. He must have, though, because he was awakened by the jingle of bells.

Father Christmas had come to make everything right!

He fell back asleep, but then sat up in bed before the sun rose, waiting under his blanket for Mama to come to him. Hand in hand they would rush into the parlour to see what magic Father Christmas had left behind.

He listened for her steps, for the rustle of her robe. He sniffed, trying to catch the sweet scent that always surrounded her.

He waited and waited. When he could no longer wait, he got out of bed to find her. Perhaps last night's stomach ache or the headache had kept her in bed.

Rushing into the Viscountess's bedchamber, he found it empty.

'Mama?' He'd called her name over and over, but only silence answered.

It could only mean she would meet him in the parlour, of course, with the fireplace already ablaze—with gifts piled around the tree as high as his nose.

Only there was no fire, there were no gifts. There was no Mama.

As it turned out, the last he ever saw of her was standing in his bedroom door, gazing at him as if he were a stranger.

From that day to this, it had been, by far, the most horrible moment of his life. At the time he had not understood that Mama's husband was a jealous man or how very controlling he was.

He knew only one thing.

Love had died. Christmas had died.

And now, in this moment, the ghost of it called to him from the parlour.

He could not possibly go in. For all that he understood this was the present day, it felt wickedly like the past.

'Ah, there you are, my lord!' Mrs Muldoon stepped up beside him. 'I've a tray of cakes here. You are just in time to help us make merry.'

The cook all but propelled him into the room with her pointed elbow.

He felt no joy in this gathering. Years of heartache grinned in the form of the tree, crushing his heart as if he were still a tender young child.

'Take it down,' he said.

Surely Felicia had not really heard those words, spoken coldly and anticipating no argument.

If Lord Scarsfeld expected there would not be one, he was greatly mistaken.

'I beg your pardon?' She turned about, deliberately taking her time. 'I am sure you are not referring to this beautiful Christmas tree which your sister and I spent the afternoon decorating.'

He stared at the lovely old ornaments as if they were about to leap from the tree and attack him.

'Take it down. Put the ornaments back in the attic.'

Clearly he was familiar with the decorations and held some animosity towards them.

'I will not.' Whatever his trouble with them was, she suspected it must have to do with something in his past.

As much as she disliked confrontation, she would not let whatever it was that had been done years ago to reach across the years and diminish Abigail's joy.

Her husband stared at her, quite obviously stunned at her refusal to do his bidding.

'Of course you will.' His brows lowered, giving him a dark, fierce expression. No doubt it was the very scowl that gave the impression of his being disagreeable. Which in the moment he was being. 'I am Scarsfeld, my word is final.'

Of all the ridiculous things she had ever heard spoken, this was near the top of the list. If her sisters could have heard it they would have giggled hysterically. Peter would have blinked in confusion.

'Perhaps when it comes to the staff, that is true.' From the corner of her eye Felicia noticed Miss Shirls cover her mouth to hide a—smile? 'But I am Lady Scarsfeld, by your own decree, might I remind you. I belong here now and I will have a Christmas tree— perhaps two of them.'

'You have no idea what—' All of a sudden his gaze shifted to Abigail sitting in a chair, her foot elevated and a bandage wrapped around it. 'What has happened?'

Wicked Christmas tree apparently forgotten, he

rushed to Abigail, going down on one knee to inspect her foot.

'Have you been hurt?' he asked even though it was obvious she had been. 'How did this happen?'

'I've twisted my ankle for the first time ever!'

Felicia thought it might have been easier for Isaiah to accept Abigail's injury had she not appeared so proud of it.

'Running on the stairs? Sliding down the banister? I've told you not leap off the couch a thousand ti—'

'She was rescuing Eloise from becoming a hawk's lunch,' Felicia blurted out in order to halt Isaiah's recitation of the ways his sister might have disobeyed him.

'I caught my foot on a branch hidden under the snow. But you will be relieved to know that Eloise is safe.'

'You ventured outside in this weather?' Isaiah's face grew the shade of a freshly bleached sheet.

Given what he had been through in nearly losing his sister once, she understood how he might feel.

'We could hardly have cut down a Christmas tree inside the house,' Abigail pointed out.

A wise and valid point, in Felicia's opinion.

'You…' He spun on his knee, pinning his attention on Felicia. 'You took my sister outside with a great storm bearing down upon us to cut down this—'

He flicked his hand at the tree as if the beautiful thing was a mere weed to be scorned.

'I forbid you to take my sister anywhere without my consent.'

'I think,' Abigail declared, clearly unaffected by her brother's temper, 'she is my sister as much as you are my brother. Therefore I will accept her permission to be equal to your forbidding.'

Oh, dear. Her words had to have cut Isaiah deeply. After all, he was the one to have raised Abigail from infancy and given his life in the cause of seeing to her well-being. At a time when he might have been in London going to the gentleman's clubs, attending balls and seeking the companionship of fine ladies, he had been raising his baby sister.

For this, Felicia greatly respected him. A fact which had nothing to do with this Christmas tree.

'Isaiah…' Felicia touched his elbow, in a gentle attempt to lead him to a chair. 'Won't you sit for a moment, have some cake and look at our tree? See how beautiful it really is?'

'Take it down,' he muttered coldly, then jerked his arm out of her grip.

He stalked out of the room in long angry-looking strides. For pity's sake, it was a wonder that sparks were not flying from his boots.

'Do not take it to heart, Sister. I, for one, do not regret this tree,' Abigail stated, her smile bright and pleased. 'It is exquisite and I adore it.'

'What a pity we shall be forced to remove it.' Mrs Muldoon shook her head.

They would not remove it, of course. Abigail had as much right to be joyful over her first Christmas tree as her brother had to snarl over it.

'We will not remove one little ornament from it,' Felicia said with a determined nod. 'In time Lord Scarsfeld will adjust to having a Christmas tree, perhaps come to enjoy it even.'

'I hope that is true. It is a beautiful tree,' Mrs Muldoon said. 'May I say, my lady, how very grateful I am that you are here? For Abigail's sake and my lord's.'

She handed Abigail a cake, then bustled from the room.

In the moment, no words could have felt more encouraging. To know that she was appreciated was what she needed to hear.

Her spirits had sunk rather low all of a sudden.

Very clearly the favour of the one person who mattered so greatly to her was not shining upon her and there was very little she could do about it.

'Abigail,' she said, turning about with a false but bright smile. 'I think we need a few more decorations on this tree. What do you say we make some?'

For all that she did not show it, the child had to be discouraged by her brother's reaction to her first Christmas tree.

Because of it, it was imperative for Felicia to remain firmly in favour of having one.

'That sounds like a great deal of fun.' She frowned while saying so. 'I have never made a decoration. I hope I will not be a failure at it.'

'Do not worry, Sister. I've made a thousand of them and will show you every trick I know.'

If only she knew enough tricks to get her husband to accept the tree.

It broke her heart, something so beautiful going unappreciated. It was not to be borne that a symbol of Christmas that ought to be a joy was causing disharmony.

Just what she was to do about it, she could not imagine. Isaiah had suffered as a child and that suffering had formed who he was today for good or for ill.

She was not as foolish as to believe it was only ill. Far more of Isaiah was good than ill. Was he not dedicated to making sure his sister did not suffer the heartache of being ripped from home and family as he had been?

There was nothing she wanted more than to help him, to bring out the happier nature in him. However, she would not do it by yielding to unreasonable demands.

'I'll just dash outside and collect some pine cones,' she said. 'We will have a grand time of it, wrapping them in the red and green ribbons I bought in the village.'

'It's getting dark, Felicia. I can wait until tomorrow to do it.'

'Unless there really is a big storm on the way. We won't be able to get them once it is upon us. We will be housebound with nothing to occupy us.'

Honestly, the thought of wild weather raging outside while remaining warm and cosy within was appealing.

Especially if she and her younger sister were creating Christmas ornaments together.

She was going to have those pine cones and some artful twigs as well. It was not horribly dark yet and she would take a lantern to gather them by.

It had grown completely dark by the time Felicia reached the grove of pines and spruce growing near the lake's edge. The copse was not far from the house, but it had taken more time than she had expected to find a cloth bag to put pine cones in and a lantern to light the way.

Stepping in among the trees, she glanced at the ground. It was still covered with the last snowfall, but she did see pine cones scattered here and there.

The moon, one moment shining brightly on the snow and the next blocked by heavy clouds, was no help in illuminating her quest.

She set the lantern on a rock. The circle of light exposed a small patch of ground where a dozen or so pine cones lay half buried.

It really was a magical setting—the snow aglitter in lamplight, the delicate etching of small animal tracks winding in and out of the circle of light. Beyond that, the great dark lake was being alternately lit and then hidden by the battle between moon and clouds.

Bending, she picked up pine cone after pine cone, placing the best in the bag and tossing less suitable ones over her shoulder.

Wind whooshed softly about. Bare branches overhead rustled, moaning and whispering to each other.

'Oh, aren't you the perfect one?' she whispered softly, not wishing to disrupt the beautiful solitude.

Glancing back at the house, seeing the windows merrily aglow in lamplight and smoke curling out of a dozen chimneys, she felt at peace.

Perhaps even at home.

The more she gazed at the stately manor, the more she felt she belonged here. She would not have thought it possible to form an attachment so quickly to a place.

There was a reason for that, of course, and it did not have to do with bricks and mortar. Rather, it had to do with the cantankerous, handsome, and confused man who owned it. Confused was the very word to describe him. Apparently, because of his childhood scars—and they were horrible—he felt he was incapable of love, yet he loved his sister quite deeply. Which only went to show his heart was not dead, but only in hiding.

Well, she would not allow him to hide from her! He might never come to love her, but she would help him heal as best she could.

She would not have believed it possible to form an attachment to her new husband so quickly, especially after the way he had behaved towards an innocent tree.

But here she was, unable to get him out of her mind even when she wanted to scold him as much as kiss him again.

She gave herself a mental shake. She had not come out here to wool gather, but to gather pine cones.

From the moment when she had spoken her wedding vows, she belonged to Scarsfeld and had a duty to see to the well-being of everyone living here.

Which was wonderful because it gave her a purpose. In the moment that purpose was to see that everyone living here had a happy Christmas.

Decorations, both the making of them and the viewing of them, added to the joy of the day.

She moved the lantern to another stone, then went to work on the pine cones revealed in its circle of light.

The bag was becoming full and, rather than constantly stooping to gather each cone, she duck-walked, dragging her treasure behind her.

Oh, my! Just there beyond the circle of light she spotted the rounded shape of the most perfect of them all.

At least it seemed so from here. But it was half-buried in snow and greatly obscured in the dark shadow of a tree trunk so it was hard to know for certain.

Since it held a great deal of promise she could hardly pass it by without a look.

Deciding not to bother with the lantern, she duck-waddled towards it, keeping the hem of her skirt tucked into the crook of her arm.

It was terribly dark in this spot. It was all she could manage to keep sight of the most lovely and perfect decoration.

Now within reach, she grabbed for it.

What? It slid neatly away from her fingers!

That was unnatural and alarming.

The only explanation for that behaviour was an unseen slope. She had to have knocked it and sent it rolling to the right a few inches.

She reached for it again. This time she plucked it up, grinning at its great size.

'Lady Scarsfeld,' rumbled a deep voice which sounded as if it were hovering over her. 'What are you doing out here in the dark?'

Her gaze focused on a boot toe. So that was what had kicked her pine cone away. She glanced sharply up.

She was correct. The voice was hovering over her—right over her since Lord Scarsfeld was bent at the waist gazing down.

This was certainly a mortifying turn of events. Not that she had done anything to be ashamed of. It was more that she must have looked beyond awkward waddling about on her haunches.

And then to not even see him hiding in the shadows! He would think her careless of her safety now.

She stood up, waggling her bag. 'I am very clearly gathering pine cones.'

'In the dead of night?'

'It is only past seven.'

'Still, dark as pitch.'

Rather like his expression, she thought.

Felicia held the bag with both hands, pleased that her gathering had been successful enough to make it so heavy.

'Only when the moon is behind the clouds,' she correctly pointed out. 'And as you can see, I do have a lantern. Have you noticed how often you come upon me unawares? Pop right out of the shadows?'

Isaiah took the bag, relieving her of the weight, but then he tossed the bag aside. It came to rest with a dozen or more cones spilled on the snow.

'Have you no sense?' Darkness hid his expression, but she didn't need to see his face to know it would look judgemental, as in 'as her husband he knew best.'

One only had to see her work scattered over the ground to know this was not true.

'More sense than to toss aside a half-hour's work.' She jabbed her finger in the direction of bag. 'Why, I ought to—'

'Felicia!' He cupped her face in his cold hands. Apparently he had come after her in such haste he had neglected to put on gloves.

Who, she wondered, but refrained from saying so aloud, was the one lacking sense?

The moon slid out from behind a cloud. Oh, dear, it

would be better had the cloud remained. She saw his expression now, flint being struck, sparks igniting his eyes. 'It might have been anyone standing behind the tree.'

She should not laugh at the thought of it. Really, she should not, but how startled would that stranger have been to have his peaceful moment ruined by someone creeping up to snatch a pine cone near his boot?

'Is there someone in particular on the premises you feel I ought to be wary of?'

'Did it not occur to you that some bearish fellow from Windermere might wander on to the estate?'

'Or from the house?'

Honestly, it had been such a lovely evening until he had come to 'rescue' her from the peril of pine cones, shifting moonlight, and whispering breeze.

His hands fell abruptly away from her cheeks. Not a moment too soon since she had been considering biting his fingers—or kissing them.

'You mock me.'

'And you discredit my intelligence.'

Not to mention setting her insides reeling until she did not know up from down, laughable from serious.

'Could you not have done this tomorrow morning?' he asked while squatting to shove the spilled pine cones back into the bag.

'As I recall it, you disclosed that a storm was going to bury us alive. If Abigail and I have any hope of making it through the catastrophe, we will need a diversion.'

'We have plenty of kindling for the fire already set in store. But if you wish, you may toss these in as freely as you like.'

Burn her pine cones? She yanked on the bag.

'Have you never seen one wrapped in ribbons and hung on the—that is, hung about the room?' she asked in order to spin the conversation away from the hated Christmas tree. 'It is the prettiest—'

'In the future, you will not come outside after dark on your own. If you wish to brave the elements, you will request my company.'

He was not an easy man to divert. Given that, she would not attempt to. Better to lead with the truth.

'I would not have come out had you not frightened us with rumours of the looming weather and—'

'It is looming.'

'And because of your unpleasant attitude towards our Christmas tree, I felt something pleasant was in order.' She yanked on the bag again, but he held it fast in his strong hand. She would not be able to peel those long, manly, fingers off it even if she tried to loosen them one by one. Especially if she tried to, since she would completely lose her focus. 'In order to restore our happy mood.'

There, she was capable of being as frank as he was. She did not care to be, but she was well able.

'Peace will be restored once you have removed the wretched tree.'

'I imagine we are in for it, then, Lord Scarsfeld.'

He spun on his heel and strode towards the house, still in possession of her bag.

Marching along the path with long—and to her mind—arrogant strides, he did not glance back at her which could only mean he was confident that she would follow.

Which meant he was about to learn that she had more pride than to meekly trail after him.

Luckily, there was more than one path back towards the house. She spun about and walked in the opposite direction he took.

Peace indeed! She had no wish to bow meekly to the bear. He was not the only one in residence whose wishes needed to be taken into account.

Only one, misguided person wanted the tree gone while a dozen others quite admired it.

'Felicia!' she heard him shout. He must have noticed she was not tagging obediently behind.

She would not give him the satisfaction of glancing his way. Instead, she ploughed along her own path, head down and determined. Because of that, she failed to see that it was blocked by a huge fallen limb and covered in a mound of snow.

There was no way around the object…or the humiliation.

With deliberate slowness, she picked her way back towards the trail Isaiah had taken.

Let him wait, shivering and probably cursing. There had been no need for him to come outside after her in the first place. Indeed, had he not, she would have been blissfully warm inside by now.

Curiously, the weather did seem uncomfortably cold all of a sudden, much more forbidding than when she had first come out.

However, now that she had set her course in motion, she must also suffer the nippy elements.

Drat it. She had suffered enough humiliation this

evening as it was. She was not going to let her pride suffer further only because she was shivering—violently.

Oh, dear. Isaiah dropped her bag, came stalking back along the path.

She started to shiver. It was cold—but more than that the tremor had to do with the man stalking towards her. He was so very—and he made her feel—she was not frightened of him, so why was she shivering?

Now, standing nose to nose with her, he puffed steaming breath into her face, then he swooped her up into his arms and carried her towards the house.

'My pine cones!' she exclaimed directly into his ear as he marched past the bag on the ground.

Without setting her down, he bent and snagged the bag. He dropped it into her lap.

Oh…my…she had never been carried by a man before and it was a very interesting sensation. It made her belly tickle, her heart speed up.

Not only that, she was so close to his neck that she could smell the enticing scent of his skin.

And she wanted to kiss it.

'Do you intend to bite me, Lady Scarsfeld? Because if you do I promise, I will bite back.'

Would he? No, he would not bite, but nip perhaps, and how nice and warm would his lips feel against her throat?

She nudged his neck with her nose, but he only groaned. She felt his arms tighten about her as his lungs expanded.

Her anger faded. A heated and very curious longing to never get out of his arms rushed in to fill its place.

Which did not, by any means, change her mind about

waging a battle to keep her Christmas tree or decorate these pine cones.

Indeed, for the sakes of everyone at Scarsfeld, she would carry on with her worthy purpose.

Chapter Nine

Staring at the Viscountess's chamber door, Isaiah wondered if he would ever have a proper night's sleep again.

Marriage was nothing like he imagined it would be, probably because he had not taken the time to imagine it. Wives, he had ignorantly assumed, were biddable souls with no desires greater than to be helpful and to please their husbands.

Such a supposition must have come from living a somewhat isolated life where the only two people to question his decisions aloud were his sister and Miss Shirls.

And now there was Felicia. What did one do with a woman who lacked common sense—who behaved in a way that put her safety at risk?

The first time he had met her she had been making wrong choices. She had been hanging from a tree, for pity's sake! Not only had she endangered herself, but Abigail as well.

If the memories haunting the Viscountess's chambers were not so painful, he would throw open the door, charge across the room and wake her and firmly explain what was, and what was not, acceptable behaviour.

But visiting old memories was not the only risk to be faced in the Viscountess's chamber. Felicia might be in bed—wearing something sheer. Or nothing at all.

He could not think of that if he was to deal with her behaviour.

What she had done earlier this evening was not acceptable. To venture out after dark was irresponsible. Anything might have happened to her.

What if she had hurt her ankle the way his sister had just done and no one had known she had gone out? The consequences might have been disastrous.

He had lived that horror once and would not do so again. It was only by God's merciful hand he had found Abigail that stormy night. Yes, six years had passed since then, but he had not fully recovered from the gut-twisting terror of what might have happened.

What if he had not looked up from his ledgers, listened to the still small voice prompting him to check on Abigail while she slept? He would never have known she'd wandered out. What if he had begun his search in the direction of the road instead of the lake?

She would not have survived. Years had passed since then but still, the sick fear he got whenever he thought of that time remained to haunt him.

Even though Abigail had survived, the 'what ifs' would not leave him alone. According to what fear suggested, history might change. He would not have checked on her and would have begun his search near the road.

Learning to put the past back where it belonged was not an easy thing for him.

What was going on in the moment was enough of a challenge.

Felicia probably thought badly of him. He had picked her up and hauled her back to the house. She would have had no way of knowing his reaction had been caused by fear more than anger.

If she thought him a beast, who would blame her? He had caused her to believe he would bite her.

If he could take that back, he would—except she had nudged him with her cold nose. He'd nearly dropped her right there and then. And if he had, he would have had to pick her up which might have involved leaning over her in a bed of snow. Which could have led him to behave in a way which would have melted the snow out from under them.

There was no denying there was something growing between him and his wife.

Before she had had the presumption to put up a Christmas tree in his house, they had been on course for a deep friendship. That could only be what it was, it was all he would allow it to be in spite of the way his temperature rose when he was within sniffing distance of her.

The tree! Even from downstairs he could smell the scent of it. To Felicia it was a pretty thing that brought only joy.

Perhaps because, unlike him, she had never lain beneath one shaking with cold and emotion.

The night his mother left he had come to the conclusion she was lost, alone in the snow and waiting for him to find her. Nothing else made any sense. The front door was not locked, so it stood to reason she had gone out—perhaps she had heard the bells like he had and gone out to see Father Christmas. Why would he not think it? He'd been only seven and it had made sense. He had hunted for her in the dark, with snow up to his knees for what seemed a long time. Defeated, he had come home, curled up under the branches of the Christmas tree. Mama was dead because he had failed to find her.

It was all he could think of that long-ago night while he cried and quaked under the decorated branches. Mama was dead. What else would keep her from being with him?

Hours later when the household began to go about their duties, they found him still weeping and shivering under the tree. After they had warmed him, drying what they could of his tears, they informed him his mother was not dead, but that her husband had come to fetch her in the night.

Although he was glad she was not dead, the news had crushed him. The person who used to love him no longer did.

Later that afternoon the butler helped him remove the decorations from the tree and pack them in a box.

The first he had seen of them since then was yesterday. It shamed him that the sight could devastate him after all these years.

He hid so many old fears behind a grim façade: unsettled by foul weather; too faint-hearted to enter his mother's chamber; dreading living alone again while at the same closing himself off to a woman who had vowed to remain with him for all time.

There was nothing he could do about the weather or about banishing the ghosts in his mother's bedchamber. But he could remove what had become the symbol of his mother's betrayal.

Before he could look too closely at the results of what he was about to do and what they would mean to anyone but him, he rushed downstairs.

Felicia would be disappointed. She was devoted to the tree and all its baubles. Abigail might be a bit distressed, but she had not had one in the past so it was unlikely she would be distraught over its loss.

Not to the degree he would be if the tree remained.

It was weak of him not to just bear having it. He understood that. None the less, it was coming down. They would make merry around the Yule log the same as they always had.

Felicia sensed something was wrong as soon as she was halfway down the stairs on her way to breakfast.

She paused, sniffed.

Her beautiful Christmas tree was gone! She felt the loss before she even rushed through the parlour entrance.

Not one needle of Abigail's perfect tree remained on the carpet.

Not only the child's perfect tree, but her only tree. One she had been injured in obtaining. Not that Abigail minded so much. The staff went above and beyond in pampering her.

Felicia stared at the bleak-looking corner of the room where the tree had reigned so cheerfully. She knew who the culprit was right off. Perhaps Isaiah was an elf, an imp or a puck. One thing he was not about to do was to get away with this bit of mischief. Surely he could put aside his dislike of the tree until after Christmas?

With luck she could have everything set to rights before Abigail came downstairs and discovered her brother's treachery.

'Mr Phillips?' she called. Having rushed past the butler a moment ago, she knew he was in the hallway. No doubt the poor fellow was anticipating her outraged reaction.

She put on a bright smile when he came into the parlour. This was no doing of his and she would not make him feel it was.

'Do you know where Lord Scarsfeld is, Mr Phillips?'

'He has gone to Windermere on business, my lady.'

'Good then. Do you know where he put the Christmas tree?'

'Indeed. He instructed me to deliver it to the woodpile, but as it turns out, Hemsworth and I only made it as far as the back courtyard.' He grinned while he spoke. 'Does my lady wish to have us bring it back inside?'

'I would be very grateful. And the ornaments?'

'Ah, Mrs Muldoon was to dispose of them. Somehow they ended back in the attic instead.'

'If you will be so kind as to bring everything back in here, I would appreciate it.'

Within half an hour the tree was restored to its rightful place. She began the process of placing the ornaments in the same places they had been, as best she could recall.

Mr Phillips was a help, grinning while giving advice.

'I apologise ahead of time for the temper Lord Scarsfeld will be in when he returns,' she said. 'I'll make certain he does not blame you for this.'

'My lord is a fair man, if I may say so. All of us in the household have become accustomed to his scowls. We do not fear them.'

That was all well and good. She felt the same way about Isaiah.

Be that as it may, she was as adamantly determined to keep this tree as he was to dispose of it.

'Would you ask Miss Shirls to keep Abigail upstairs until I finish here? I would rather she did not know about this.'

The one and only reason Isaiah had married her was to protect Abigail.

She took that obligation to heart. If it meant protecting her from the not so lovely side of her brother's nature, so be it.

For all that Abigail held her own where Isaiah was concerned, this battle had to do with Christmas joy.

Now that she was lady of the manor, Felicia would do the fighting.

Isaiah's business in Windermere had gone on longer than he expected it to.

It would have been wise to spend the night at one of the inns in the village, but it was already beginning to snow and he did not wish to become stranded here.

The last thing he wanted was for Scarsfeld to have to deal with a crisis and for him to be away from home.

If the icy gusts pummelling his back on the ride

home was an indication of things to come, he had made the correct choice.

The one bright spot in the weather was that, if it was as bad as people were expecting, the Penfields would be prevented from arriving at his front door.

After delivering his horse into the care of the stableman, Isaiah leaned into the wind and made his way to the house.

It was late and the staff had already retired to their rooms when he came inside. He was surprised to see fire glow spilling into the hall from the parlour.

Surprised and grateful. The journey back had left him half-frozen. It was beyond gratifying to be home.

Smiling in anticipation of warming himself before the flames, he strode into the parlour.

The breath he had been inhaling snagged in his throat, nearly choking him.

It was back! Unbelievably, the Christmas tree he had ordered sent to the woodpile, the ornaments he had consigned to the rubbish heap, were back!

Someone had disobeyed his orders. He did not have to waste time wondering who.

The pretty culprit slept upon a pile of quilts on the floor in front of the merrily mocking tree. Her knees were bent, the curve of her hip and her long limbs halfway under the branches.

Her long, exposed limbs! With her frilly sleeping gown rucked up over her knees, she still managed to appear a vision of innocence. Perhaps it was because of the way she tucked her fingers beneath her cheek in slumber.

It was hard to credit, but he found himself standing in front of a Christmas tree with a smile on his face.

Something was very off, he could not possibly be feeling anything tender in this moment—not in front of this symbol of ruin.

What was more, he had better not make the mistake of considering her his own, personal gift. For all that she resembled a tasty confection, the woman was a warrior. One who had declared war upon him.

For that was clearly what she had done. He could see it in his mind, how she must have smiled sweetly at his staff, convincing them to do her bidding instead of his.

Dash it! Just looking at her made him want to do her bidding instead of his. Not in this case, though. Were it anything but this bitter reminder of loss, he would gladly give her what she wanted.

'I'll go with you to gather pine cones,' he mumbled. 'I'll help you hang them from every rafter in the house, but I will not—'

Suddenly her eyes opened.

'Truly?' She sat up, blinking at him while she casually reached up to lift the strap of her gown back up to her shoulder. But it was a thin strap, a length of lace which still left her shoulders exposed, and the soft-looking skin of her neck and…and the—

He had to look away.

His wife wielded weapons he was helpless against.

'You defied me, Lady Scarsfeld.'

'You might say so.' She shrugged her shoulders. He was caught for a moment, wondering if her skin resembled satin or velvet. Whichever it was, the sight made his stomach flip. 'But then I might say that you under-mined me and my position as Viscountess.'

She was correct. He had done that. He had been so set on getting rid of the tree, he had not considered that.

Even so...

'You do not understand.'

'You look cold, Isaiah. Go and warm yourself by the fire and tell me what it is that I do not understand.'

He did what she said because he was cold, but more than that he was also hot. He needed to put distance be-tween himself and what she was barely wearing.

'Do you not have a robe?'

'Of course I do.'

If he had any doubt that she was using her feminine wiles against him, it vanished when she made no at-tempt to reach for it and cover herself.

She was waiting for him to speak, but he stared at her, struck mute and within a breath of surrendering, of laying bare the details of his sorry past. But he could not quite and so silence lay heavy between them.

She shattered it by saying, 'You will be relieved to know that Abigail never knew her tree went missing.'

'Do you think she will be terribly upset when she finds it gone in the morning?' Because he did intend to have it removed again.

Felicia's hair was loose. He just now noticed how one red strand curled at the spot on her throat where her pulse tapped in quick rhythm. A reminder that he had wondered about biting her there, in that very spot.

'She will not find it gone in the morning, so you need not worry that she will be anything but pleased.'

'My word is—'

'If you persist in this nonsense, your word will cause disappointment for everyone in this household. Do you honestly feel that one man's feelings are to be taken into account ahead of everyone else's?'

'Indeed, yes, if that man is the Viscount. And so far no one has complained about the lack of a tree in the house.' He cast a frown at an ornament he and his mother had fashioned when he was three years old.

Except for Abigail. She had asked for a tree.

'No one dared to,' Felicia said.

'Except you. You dare to.'

'Clearly someone must.'

'You risk a lot for the sake of that thing.'

'Not for the tree's sake alone, Husband. For your sake.'

Ah! Now he had her.

'If you mean what you say, then you will help me take it down.' Haul it outside and burn it along with every heartbreaking decoration clinging to its branches.

'It is because I mean it that I will not.' She reached for her robe, shrugged it over her shoulders. 'Come, sit beside me.'

No, the last time he was that close to a Christmas tree love had died. To sit again among evergreen branches, the ornaments which had been so special now staring at him, mocking the bond he had shared with his mother, would suffocate him.

He crossed his arms over his chest, staring down at his opponent in this battle of wills. He unsheathed his sharpest expression, pointing it at her as if to slay her point of view. To his surprise, he did not see answering combat in her eyes. Neither did he see surrender.

She had called him husband. The expression in her beautiful green eyes said she had not spoken the endearment idly. There was not a single weapon she might have drawn against him more powerful than that word.

'Isaiah…' she patted the quilt '…sit with me. Help me understand why you hate this tree.'

He did not know how she could understand a moment of it, having grown up all smiles and laughter as she had. But if speaking with her would eliminate her objections when he took the tree away, he would sit.

As long as the tree was gone by dawn, he would tell her whatever she wished to hear.

'What do you need to understand?'

He sat down, folding his legs beneath him, preparing to withstand the siege. So he told himself. If he was really doing that, he would not be sitting so close that he could smell whatever flowery scent she had bathed in. He would have put enough space between them that he could not feel the heat of her skin nipping—battering, rather—his defences.

'What is it that makes you act like someone you are not?'

He nearly gasped at the emotional impact of that question. He did it to prevent anyone from seeing inside him as she was so clearly doing right now.

Oddly, because it was Felicia searching him out, he was not fighting it as hard as he might have been. Feeling her probing his heart made him want to run away from her—but, oddly enough, towards her, too.

He would never confess it, but if someone—if Felicia—looked past the thorny barrier he had erected about himself and cared for him anyway, well, he might respond to that in a way he should not.

He might care back.

Dash it, he already cared for her. How could he deny it without being a liar?

She really was the most endearing person he had ever met. Sweet, caring and cheerful, but not without a dash of stubbornness—she was everything he was not.

One did not have to look deeply to note the staff were falling in love with her. The Christmas tree would be on the woodpile destined to be kindling for the Yule log if that were not the case.

'What makes you certain I am not exactly the person I look like?'

Because she clearly did not think so. No one looked at another with tenderness if they were shaking in their socks in fear of their crusty temperament.

He would know if she was shaking since she was not wearing anything on her feet and her slim, fascinating toes were curling then and relaxing in apparent contentment.

It could only be assumed she was more at ease with this conversation than he was.

It did not matter. Lady Scarsfeld could appear as tranquil as Eloise did while lying in a sunny window, but the freshly scented tree looming over him would still be gone before daylight.

'I have seen how you are with your sister. That is who you are, Isaiah. All the rest is bluster to hide it. What I would like to know is why you do it?'

'I would not expect you to understand. How could you having grown up as you have? From what you say, your family has always been a devoted one. Not every-one has had your advantage.'

And there was the truth, uttered with a bitter edge to his voice, an edge that she did not deserve to hear.

No doubt she would rise from the floor at the insult, rush to her chamber and give him time to dispose of the tree.

'Do you resent the way I grew up?'

Wait! Was that compassion lurking in the turn of her lips?

'I can understand it if you do. Life has not been fair to you.'

Surely she was not reaching for his hand to give it a brief squeeze.

'I'm sorry. I spoke poorly. I do not resent the way you grew up. But I do envy it. I wish I could look at your tree, see it as a joyful thing and sing carols around it. I will admit, this is something you and Abigail ought to have.'

'Let's put that aside for a moment.' Because she fully meant to have this tree. She stated so, not with words, but by the expression in her eyes. 'How would you rather have your sister grow up? Do you want her memories of these years with you to be lacking joy? Or rather, remember them with joy? Do you want her to feel she grew up happy in spite of you? Or that she found happiness in her days because of you?'

'Abigail is happy!'

Of course she was. Had he not spent his life making sure she was? Had he not married in order to keep it that way?

'Shall we put it to a test?' She reached behind her

and plucked an ornament from the tree. She held it to the lamplight, turning it this way and that to catch and reflect sparkles on the decorations he and his mother had pasted on it. 'I will help you take down the tree and remove it from the house.'

He suspected her words were a trap in which he was neatly ensnared.

Carefully, she placed the glass ball in his hand.

'We will know how happy Abigail is when she comes downstairs in the morning. Both of us will be waiting right here so we can judge whether she minds the tree being gone or not.'

Damn it! Of course she was going to mind.

'I say, toss that ornament into the fireplace. It would make as good a start as any.'

He ought to take her up on the challenge, for clearly that was what it was.

Tossing the ball from hand to hand, he stared at it.

'Here, I will do it.' She snatched the blue orb from him, lifting her arm.

Something twinkled in the depth of the glass. The sparkle reflected a memory of his mother's smile, of her kiss when she told him how proud she was of his creative work.

Before he could think better of it, he grabbed it out of Felicia's fingers. Quickly, before he could change his mind, he placed it back on the tree.

'Would you have done it?' he asked.

'I would not have. No more than you will destroy Abigail's Christmas tree knowing that, by doing so, you will break her heart.'

'There is too much that you do not understand.'

'You said so before and I asked you to tell me why I do not.'

Wiping his hands across his face, he sighed deeply within himself. Looking at her, trying to see behind her thoughts the way she so easily read his, he wondered if he could tell her what he had never told another person.

'For me, Felicia, love died the Christmas my mother left me. The last I saw of her she was standing in my bedroom doorway, looking at me as if she did not know who I was. I wonder if she was maybe looking through me as if she was already gone. She sneaked away in the night without a goodbye. I lay down under the Christmas tree, looking through my tears at these ornaments, remembering how we had made each one. All of them have a story. I cannot bear to look at them.' He closed his eyes, pressing the lids hard together to keep from seeing it all again. 'You look at this tree and see joy. I look at it and I am reminded that I will never love anyone again. I could not bear the loss.'

There, he had confessed it. The world had not collapsed around him. He felt fingers in his hair, gently stroking from temple to the curve of his ear.

'But you do love someone, Isaiah. You love Abigail. You would not be sitting here enduring the tree if you did not.'

Yes, he did—and he might lose her.

'You also love your mother.'

At those words he opened his eyes, staring hard at Felicia. While she was right about many things, she was not right about that.

'If I do hold an ounce of love for the woman, I do not

wish to. She buried a little boy's heart with her own two hands. The last thing I want is to resurrect it.'

'Then why did you not shatter the ornament?'

'It would have been a mess for the servants to deal with in the morning.'

'That, yes. But why else?'

'Felicia, you have neatly pointed out my duty here. I love Abigail and, in order to make her happy, I must not destroy her tree. Now, if you have some magic to help me deal with having to keeping it, I would be happy to know what it is.'

What kind of smile was that?

She did have something!

He greatly feared what sorcery she had in mind.

Chapter Ten

'I have an idea, only. There is no magic to it.'

In fact, she had drawn on all the magic she could expect to in one lifetime simply getting him to leave Abigail's tree in place.

He shifted his position, inching slightly closer to her, inclining his head towards hers as if expecting some great and mysterious wisdom to spout from her lips.

'What?' he asked, his brows lowered and his expression half fearful of what she might say.

'It is a simple idea, Isaiah, and logical. We must find a way to replace your bitter feelings for this Christmas tree with happy ones.'

'Simple? Logical? Do you believe I can put away what my mother did?'

'No. And you should not. But perhaps balance the hurt with understanding?'

He sat up straight, gazing at her as if she were a madwoman.

'After what she did? I do not know what there is to understand. I am raising a child. I know what that commitment means. There is nothing that could make me choose to live apart from Abigail.'

'As my presence here attests to.' In spite of the fact that he had kissed her, she had freely entered into a marriage of convenience. She should not hope for more than that and yet she did. The truth was the truth and sitting next to her husband wearing nothing but her nightgown clearly pointed that out. If only he would touch her—but that was something to think of later. 'But just for a moment, let's stand in the place of your mother, see the world as she might have.'

'I would rather not.'

'Being a man you probably could not anyway. But follow her through my eyes, Isaiah.'

He did not look pleased to be doing so, but neither did he leap up and walk away in a huff.

'I am the happiest woman on the planet. I adore my husband and have just given him the most beautiful and amazing son. I am certain she thought it to be true so you may put your frown away. You know in your heart she did. Then, a short time later, I am the saddest woman on the planet. My husband, my best friend, has died. Oh, but I still have my baby. I will pour all my love into him.'

'She did do that. It was why what came later nearly killed me.'

'It nearly killed me, too. You see, I was a young woman suddenly all alone in the world. We had run out of money and I had no one to turn to. Society expected me to remarry. So I wed a man who seemed an ideal match. For both of us.'

'Seemed, but he was far from ideal in the end.'

'It was too late to do anything about it then. You will remember how he was heavy handed, cruel to me and to you. When, after a time, he decided you should grow up at Scarsfeld, it was an answer to my prayers. At least one of us would be safe from him. At first he allowed me to visit you?'

Isaiah nodded. 'Short visits which became fewer and fewer until she never came again.'

'It broke my heart, you have to know it did.' Standing in Lady Penfield's slippers was not an easy thing to do. Felicia felt tears pressing behind her eyes. 'But I was fairly beaten down by then. I closed my heart. I refused to feel anything.'

'I did see that deadness in her soul on that last Christmas Eve. Your imagination is more than accurate.'

Oddly so. Her emotions were as engaged in this recitation as her imagination was.

'After many years I did give him the child he wanted. But he died of...?'

'Of an apoplexy, the lawyer told me. It was the week before my sister was born.'

'Yes, it was before he knew the baby was a girl and not an heir. I was glad he never knew. I was so weak from giving birth, I knew I would not be the one to raise my pretty Abigail so I sent her to you. But do not fear that I was unhappy in that moment, Isaiah, because there was something that I learned, from you and from my baby girl. Children are the ones who make everything right. You cannot regret a past that has brought them into the world.'

For some reason tears were slipping down her

cheeks. It felt almost as if Juliette had been there, a guide through her past.

'Isaiah, I feel that if your mother were here speaking to you, she would want you to understand that she always loved you.'

He was silent for a very long time, staring at the fireplace. His forearms rested atop his bent knees while he curled his fingers into fists.

'I do not know about that,' he finally said, brushing a spot on his cheek. 'Those might have been her feelings, but we are only playing a game. But one thing you said did strike me, Felicia. It's to do with my sister. Had the past not been as it was, she would not be here. I think she is worth it all.'

'It is a start, then.'

He swung his head to look at her. 'I'm still going to need to make some very good memories if I am to gaze upon this thing without feeling sick.'

'It stands to reason.' It was up to her to supply a good memory to ease the bitter. She glanced about. 'Are there any games in here we could play? Chess, perhaps?'

'If you would rather go to bed, you may. The floor cannot have been a comfortable place to sleep.' Reaching across the short distance between them, he squeezed her hand, then smiled. 'I promise not to destroy your Christmas tree while you sleep.'

'Do you realise what you just did?' And left her heart all dizzy over it.

'I made a promise. Do not worry. I will keep it.'

'But you smiled when you gave it. You grinned and said "Christmas tree" at the same time.'

'An accident, clearly.' Then why was he still smiling?

'I think our tactic is working.'

'I do not know what memory we created to erase the old.'

'We simply spoke to each other, openly and truthfully the way friends do.'

Now, fully understanding his wounds and how he believed that love had died for him, she did not feel it was the time to tell him all of her heart, how a moment ago she had concluded she wanted more of his.

A time would come, she hoped, when she could convince him love had not died.

'Chess?' she asked.

'I'll get the board.' Isaiah stood up and walked out of the room.

When he returned he carried the chess game and half a dozen buns.

'I stopped in at the kitchen. At this hour Mrs Muldoon is asleep so these are not warm with doilies underneath. But I thought we needed sustenance for our endeavour, don't you agree?' He sat down beside her and set up the game.

She could not help but be encouraged since he might have more easily set the game on a table next to the window and not under the tree he detested.

He had beaten her twice, then she beat him once before she yawned.

'It is very late,' he pointed out. 'We should retire.'

He was correct. They ought to have done so some time ago, she thought while he gathered the game pieces and put them away. The problem was, they would now part company.

She truly did not want to.

He stood up, then reached his hand down for her. Naturally she took it, making sure to take a long time to come to her feet.

She need not have because he did not let go of her hand. Instead he lifted her fingers to his lips and kissed them.

'You said something earlier, Felicia—I need to make something clear about it.'

'What is it?'

He looked into her eyes, his expression unguarded. She wanted to throw herself into his arms and hug him. With his barrier down was he about to let her into his heart? Did she dare hope it? She must, because her heart was beating madly and it would not be doing so for no reason.

'It has to do with what you said—about being my wife. When I said I would do anything for Abigail, you replied that it was the reason you were here, or words to that effect. Do you recall it?'

'Yes, and it is why I'm here. The reason is no secret between us.'

'You also called me Husband.'

'You are that, are you not? And a rather good one since you have promised not to harm the Christmas tree.'

'I must have been half-insane when I vowed it. But vow it I did—Felicia, the bit about Abigail being the reason you are here? It was true in the beginning, but no longer. I will admit I proposed marriage to you only as a means of protecting my sister. What I could not see at the time was that luck was smiling upon me when you fell out of that tree. I am grateful, but that is not quite right since I have always been grateful—what I am is happy. Felicia, I am glad you are Lady Scarsfeld. Even if we are not successful in keeping Abigail with us, I am thankful you will still be here.'

All right, that was something close to what she wished to hear and it warmed her through.

'I'm glad, too.'

For him to say he was glad she was Lady Scarsfeld was wonderful, but not the same thing as him being glad she was his wife. Being a wife implied a certain intimacy, whereas Lady of the manor was simply a title.

'And we will be successful, Isaiah.'

'In everything, is what I mean. Home is where the heart is, so they say. I hope it is true for you. I want you to feel this is where you belong.'

'I am beginning to.'

'Perhaps you require a good memory as much as I do. In order to help the process along?'

He slid both of his arms around her back, slowly drawing her towards him.

'One can never have too many good memories,' she whispered close to his lips and closer, she thought, to his heart.

The game apparently forgotten, he dropped it. Playing pieces clattered on the wood floor.

Oh, my—she leaned into him, felt all soft and gooey. Completely melted by his kiss.

Whose good memory was this?

Hers? Indeed, it was. She felt so—so consumed she could not quite put the feeling to words. Of course, no words were required, only that she lean into her husband and let her senses soak in the essence of Isaiah.

His heart beat hard against hers. She was engulfed in muscle, hot breath and masculinity.

This memory was not hers alone. Oh, no, it was so much more than that.

It was their memory to be cherished together.

And what was more, it had happened in front of the Christmas tree.

Please let him be drinking in this moment without the bitter taste of the past to poison it.

Coming downstairs to breakfast the next morning, Isaiah wondered if last night had been a mistake. It did not feel like one. In fact, he had slept better than he had since receiving the letter from Lord Penfield. Even upon waking he did not feel the weight of fear pressing upon him as he often did.

Following his nose towards the breakfast room, he wondered if the contentment he felt in the moment would hold if he turned aside towards the parlour.

Looking at the tree might change everything, cast him back to his normal, ill-humoured self.

He would find that out later—at the moment, the scent of bacon and the sound of his sister's laughter drew him towards the breakfast room.

It hit him hard, realising that, had he acted on his own selfish motivation and destroyed the tree, Abigail would not be laughing.

It hit him harder, knowing that, if not for his bride's intervention, it would be weeping instead of laughter that he heard.

Rounding the corner and entering the room, he saw Felicia and Abigail together, their heads bent while giggling over something.

Isaiah had raised his sister all these years and never understood that she needed a close bond with a woman. All these years she had been lacking and he had never known it.

'Good morning, Isaiah.' Felicia glanced up at him, her smile twinkling and cheerful. 'I trust you slept well?'

All these years, he thought, while watching the curve of the smile meant just for him—all these years, how could he have failed to recognise his own need of a woman?

Not a carnal need, he did not mean that as much as he meant the close tie that came from bonded hearts.

Perhaps he had not known it because he had not known her. Felicia was the only person who had ever cared enough to scale his wall.

What he could only wonder was, how did she feel about him now that she had?

He picked up a plate and filled it with food from the sideboard. Sitting down, he wondered if his wife was correct in her game of easing bad memories by gathering new ones. Just watching his sister and Felicia chatting, laughing, was making a good memory.

'How is your foot, Abigail?'

'Much improved. I slid down the banister this morning to avoid putting too much pressure on it.'

The first thing to come to his mind was to scold her. Sliding down the banister was a safety risk and forbidden.

Just in time he recalled what Felicia had told him about what he wished his sister to remember during her life with him.

A scolding was not the thing.

Felicia rose from the table all of a sudden. She hurried to the window.

'It is snowing!' She clapped her hands. 'We should go out and have a snowball fight.'

'Oh! Let's do!' Abigail started to rise and then winced.

'You are hurt and a big storm is coming. We shall remain safely indoors.'

It was a lucky thing he was here to add a voice of reason to the discussion. Left to their own choice, his women would dash outside in spite of the danger.

'But it is not big yet, which is all the more reason to go out now,' Abigail persisted. 'We ought to get fresh air and exercise while we are able to.'

'You are not able to,' he pointed out since she was ignoring the fact that it was painful for her to walk.

'I am if you carry me out and set me in a chair. I can easily form my weapons while I sit.'

'Are you forgetting what a target you will make?' In spite of his reservations he was beginning to imagine the possibilities. 'Sitting chairbound and unable to dodge out of the way of my assault?'

'Your sister and I will be a team!' Felicia rang for their coats. 'She will throw her weapons at you while I deflect the ones you throw at her!'

'Two against one?'

If this was going to happen, he had best be out there with them. For one thing, he would be the judge of when it was time to come in, but, more than that, he did not want to miss a second of it.

'It has been pointed out,' Felicia stated, her eyes alight with mischief, 'that you are stronger than you appear.'

Within a quarter of an hour, the three of them were bundled up and ready to go.

He carried Abigail. Even in layers of clothing she was light which served to remind him that, in spite of her rather large personality, she was but a child.

'Thank you for taking me out to play,' She hugged his neck. 'This will be the best snowball fight we have ever had.'

'Why do you think so?'

'Because Felicia is here. We will have great fun.'

'You and I have always had fun.'

'Yes, but now that we have her it will be better.'

Mr Phillips hurried past them, carrying a chair. He set it down a safe distance from the lake.

Carefully, Isaiah placed her in the chair. She tugged his sleeve when he would have gone off to form his weapons.

'I only meant to say I'm glad you married her. Scarsfeld has never been so happy a place as it is now.'

'I can only agree.'

It was happier. He had yet to decide if that condition comforted him or frightened him.

What would happen if he fully let go of his heart, trusted it completely to another person? It would be a great risk, yet had he not already given Felicia a part of his heart? So far nothing hurtful had come of it.

'Be ready for defeat, Brother!'

'Come, Felicia.' Isaiah plucked on her coat sleeve. 'We shall craft our weapons together.'

There were a few mounds of good snow close by, but he led her towards the furthest one.

Something was on his mind and he needed her opinion on it.

That was something in itself. All his life he had made his decisions, for good or for ill, on his own. It felt good to be able to count on another person's advice. Especially when it was given by his wife, whom he was coming to believe was a very wise lady.

'I need to know what you think of something, Felicia,' he said, reaching down to scoop up a handful of snow.

'As you might have guessed by now, I am accomplished at giving opinions.'

'This is advice more than that.'

'What is it, Isaiah?'

They bent and scooped while they talked, pounding snow into balls and stacking them.

'You know I never told Abigail why her aunt and uncle are coming. But, in fact, I did not tell her they are coming at all. Do you think I ought to? They will be here in two days so I cannot put it off for ever.'

Felicia smashed a snowball on his head with a great mischievous smile. In doing so she made their conversation appear to be competitive as would suit the game they were about to play.

'I think she has to know they are coming for a visit. Otherwise she will wonder why you did not tell her about it. But as for their reason for coming? We will pray she never discovers it.'

'Very well. I will tell her about it after I beat the two of you in this game.'

'Abigail!' Felicia called while carrying over their share of snowballs. 'Your brother thinks he is going to slay us in this battle.'

His sister's laugh was young, carefree. He could listen to it for ever. He only hoped nothing, or no one, would ever change that. He only hoped that the fact he was married and therefore a stable family man would be enough to discourage the Penfields from taking her away. That they would put her well-being over their desire to raise her in London.

Abigail pitched the first ball and hit him in the shoulder.

Felicia prepared for his retaliation by standing in front of her partner, shielding her by waving her arms and dancing about on her toes.

Oh, yes. This added twist to the game was going to be great fun.

Taking aim, he launched his shot, hitting Felicia in the knee. Next Abigail got him in the hip. Then he landed a ball on Felicia's upraised fist where she was about to launch a blow at him.

Felicia and Abigail were laughing to the point of being breathless.

It startled him to hear his own laugh. Until this moment he had not been sure he still had one.

Apparently it startled his opponents, too, for all action stopped while they stared at him, jaws hanging agape.

Their mistake. It gave him an instant to snatch up a ball in each hand.

One of them, a purposefully soft one, hit Felicia square in the nose. While she swiped the snow from her face he delivered the other to Abigail's lap.

'I win!' he shouted, feeling exultant in victory. One defeating two was a great triumph.

'We surrender!' Abigail's sly grin belied her words.

Felicia strode forward, hands behind her back.

'Congratulations, Lord Scarsfeld,' she said, then shoved two snowballs in his face. 'Own your loss!'

Blinking through ice crystals, he grabbed for her and missed. She spun neatly away, dancing on her toes.

There would be payment for this treachery! He was vaguely aware of hearing his sister laughing while he lunged after his opponent.

Felicia was quick, he would give her that. Each time he reached for her she bounded adroitly beyond his grasp.

'Do you concede defeat, Isaiah?' she asked, breathless.

Ah, here was where his superior strength would gain him the win! 'Do you?'

'I am far too fleet of foot to be caught by the lumbering likes of you!'

And so he lunged, taking aim at her middle. The trouble was, the superior strength he had mentally boasted of also gave him the greater weight. It would be a hollow victory if he injured his wife to achieve it.

Mid-fall he flipped her so that she ended up on top of him, which made it falsely appear the victory was hers.

Winded, her breath puffing in his face, she asked, 'Which of us is the winner?'

'We should vote on it!' Abigail called.

'Yes—vote,' she muttered, her breath changing from exertion to something more breathy—more intimate.

'Ha! A guarantee of my loss. I do not agree to it.'

One of them needed to make a move to rise. It was not as if they were alone. Yet here they were, lying breast to breast in the snow, gazing at one another.

There was more going on here than met the eye. Yes, whichever of them got up first would be admitting defeat, but that was not all of it. Something was changing between them that his sister would not be aware of—at least he did not think she would be.

Something began to change in the weather, too. Snowflakes blew sideways instead of drifting gently down. Wind picked up, moaning through the tree tops and making winter-bare branches scratch together.

It was time to go inside. Not because of the change in the weather, but because of the change in him.

If it were not for the fact that Abigail was sitting only feet away, he would—

Ah, but she was there and peering at them with a strange little smile.

Also, the conservatory door opened.

No doubt Miss Shirls was going to demand they come inside. He was going to have the devil of a time explaining this 'game' as it was.

But why should he be obliged to explain anything? Felicia was his wife.

'This is a good game. We ought to play it again,' he said, revelling in the heat of her breath on his face. It felt extra comforting since he was growing cold from taking the brunt of the snow.

'Oh, indeed. We need a rematch in order to know who the winner truly was.'

He was the winner. This was one more memory his wife had presented him. Another small step out of the dark place he'd chosen to keep his heart.

A throat cleared. Someone gasped.

A second later Mr Phillips announced, 'Lord and Lady Penfield, my lord.'

Here? Now!

'I suppose you ought to let me up now, Felicia.'

'Indeed.' She raised up, casting a glace over her shoulder at the Earl and the Countess. 'We are on the same team now.'

Even with the frowns being cast down from the terrace, Isaiah could not recall when anything had made him feel better.

Preceding everyone into the parlour, Mr Phillips's expression appeared pinched.

Of course it would, Felicia thought. The guests had arrived days ahead of schedule. The staff would not be prepared for them.

Miss Shirls, ever in charge, had acted swiftly and swept Abigail away the instant they stepped inside the house. She insisted the child must be changed into a dry gown. It was interesting how the governess all but shielded her from the guests' view. It was almost as if she knew they were not here to share holiday cheer.

If only Isaiah had informed Abigail they were coming. How on earth was he going to explain why he had not?

'Welcome to Scarsfeld. It is good to see you, Penfield.' Isaiah extended his hand in greeting to the rigid-looking man. To be fair he probably could not look any other way because of his nose. Sharp, as much beak as nose, it would slice the most earnest of smiles.

'Lady Penfield.' Isaiah turned his attention to the woman who looked like a fluffy round sparrow to her husband's hawk. 'I am delighted you came to visit.'

Of course Felicia knew he was not delighted. They surely knew it, too, because of what passed as Isaiah's smile.

While Mr Phillips helped Felicia off with her wet coat, the Penfields' gazes swung her way. They must be wondering who it was that Isaiah had been carousing with in the snow, right in front of Abigail's innocent eyes! They could not know it had been but a game.

'Allow me to introduce my wife, Lady Scarsfeld.'

Both of them had to look up at her while offering a greeting.

Casting a loving smile at Isaiah, Felicia was reminded how glad she was not to have to look down at him. All right, there was the inch, but it did not signify.

She took a steadying breath. Let this show begin, then. Although, given how her heart spun a dizzy jig when Isaiah smiled back at her, clearly it was not all for show.

'Welcome to Scarsfeld!' Felicia held out both of her hands to Lady Penfield, making sure her smile of welcome would make up for Isaiah's lack of one. 'How perfectly wonderful that you were able to make it. We feared the weather would prevent your visit.'

'As did we,' Lady Penfield answered. 'It is why we travelled early. I hope our untimely arrival will not inconvenience you.'

'Not at all. We are only happy you were able to come. Christmas spent with family is ever so much better than spent alone, do you not agree?'

Felicia wished Isaiah would stop trying to smile. Their guests were going to feel as unwelcome as they actually were.

'Oh, I do.' Lady Penfield's smile showed such relief that Felicia felt more kindly towards her. 'Given the reason we are here, I thought—well, you might not welcome us.'

'Oh, but you are family through Abigail. She would be grieved to think there were hostile feelings between us.'

'Scarsfeld,' Lord Penfield stated from where he had taken a position in front of the hearth, 'I did not hear that you had married.'

'It was a quiet affair.'

'And convenient, I suspect.'

'Oh, dear,' Lady Penfield muttered for Felicia's ears alone. 'My husband is not as beastly as he appears. Truly, we are overjoyed to hear your happy news.'

Isaiah opened his mouth, probably to return vocal fire. Felicia hurried over, insinuating herself under his arm. As she had expected, tension rippled through his chest.

'Delightfully convenient.' With a half-lidded gaze at

Isaiah, she sighed. 'Once one is smitten it is foolhardy to postpone one's vows.'

'Only trouble can come of it, otherwise,' Lady Penfield agreed.

'I, for one, believe this marriage is a sham. Carried out in order to make my niece's life here appear favourable.'

'Do not be a dolt, Henry. It is rude of you to suggest such a thing. Look at the two of them and tell me you do not remember how it was to be young and in love.'

Oddly enough, the hawk blushed. Lord Penfield and Lord Scarsfeld had some things in common. Perhaps there was a chance for them to rise above the ill will sparking between them.

Peter would accuse her of looking at things through rose-coloured spectacles. Yet it was the Christmas season and unlikely things—wonderful things—might happen.

Right behind her the tree, still standing and all a-glitter, was proof of it.

'Her life here has always been favourable, my lord.' How brightly could one smile without freezing one's face? Felicia wanted to know. 'You shall see it for yourself soon. Abigail is a delight, which of course is a credit to her brother. I have rarely seen siblings so devoted to one another.'

That part was easy to say since it was the truth.

It was also not what their guests wanted to hear. It would be easier to remove Abigail from her home if they believed it was for her own good.

Felicia's job was to make them see the truth, to understand it was in Abigail's best interests for her to remain at home with her brother, which meant she needed to do what she could about softening her husband's image. This would involve appearing to be completely besotted with him, which was not so far from the truth.

'You must be weary from travel,' Felicia said. 'It looks as if you arrived in the nick of time. Just look at that snow out of the window! It is growing heavier by the moment.'

It truly was. Great sheets of white sailed past the windows. It was difficult to see ten feet beyond the glass.

'We saw it developing while we were still in Windermere,' Lord Penfield remarked. 'I must say, I was relieved to arrive at your door when we did.'

'The worsening weather all but pounced upon us. We were involved in a snowball fight and had neglected to notice how hard the snow was coming down. Isaiah...' she said, giving him her full attention. 'It was a lucky thing Abigail and I defeated you as quickly as we did.'

It was important to establish from the start that Scarsfeld was a fun place for a child to grow up and what was more fun than a battle with snowballs?

Isaiah arched his brows at her, his smile rare and, she felt, genuine. 'As I recall it, we agreed upon a rematch.'

'I hoped you had forgotten that part.' She patted his cheek as if it were the most natural thing to do, as if he were the most fun loving of souls.

He, in turn, kissed her cheek. It felt so lovely even though she knew it to be play acting. But he had kissed her cheek before, and her lips, had done it with only the two of them to know it. Dared she hope this was not play acting?

'We will have our rematch,' he stated.

In that moment, tea and sandwiches arrived. Felicia might have known Mrs Muldoon would have begun preparing when the coach was first spotted coming down the lane.

With a sweep of her hand that was sure to show off her beautiful wedding band, Felicia indicated that they should sit in front of the fireplace where flames leapt in friendly welcome.

It could not hurt that the scent of the Christmas tree added a heart-warming mood to the parlour.

With any luck the undercurrent of hostility between the men would ease in the homely setting.

At least Felicia sensed no mood of antagonism in Lady Penfield. With luck the woman might be made an ally rather than an opponent.

'A rematch we shall have, then,' Felicia announced, returning to the paused conversation. 'If our guests agree to participate, you will have aid this time, Isaiah. It will be you and Lord Penfield matched against me, Abigail, and Lady Penfield.'

'My word! That sounds like grand fun.' Lady Penfield clapped her hands. 'Oh, Henry, let's hope the weather clears.'

'Of course, my dear.' Lord Penfield's smile at his wife was affectionate. It was clear to see he doted upon her. 'I shall hope just that.'

What a blessing to discover the Earl had a softer side. All it needed was a bit of cultivation.

Perhaps there was hope that, in the end, the couple would act in Abigail's best interest and not their own.

Isaiah could finally breathe. With tea finished and the Penfields retired to their suite of rooms, he felt he could act himself—whoever that was. The past few hours had revealed a side of him he had thought lost.

Playtime in the snow with his sister and his wife had been genuine fun. How long had it been since he had allowed himself to give over to joy with anyone but Abigail? It was when life had been good with his mother.

Very clearly he had married sunshine personified. If only he could trust that storm clouds would not come racing in to snuff it out. The truth was, he had known her so briefly, how could he be aware of every facet to her character?

Just as true, even though their acquaintance had been brief, she had given him no reason to doubt she was who she seemed to be. Day by day, even hour by hour, he was becoming ever more fond of her. Her smile and the happy sound of her laughter took up the greater part of his attention. He was eager to find her in order to discuss the conversation he'd just had with his sister, to discover what her opinion of their guests was.

He did not find her in the parlour guarding her precious Christmas tree, nor was she in the kitchen watching Mrs Muldoon buzz about.

Turning down the corridor that led to the library, he heard someone singing 'Away in a Manger.' He followed the pretty, if off-key, rendition down the hallway.

As soon as he opened the door, she looked up from the book lying open on her lap. As always, she greeted him with a sunny, welcoming smile. All of a sudden he barely minded the blizzard pounding the estate.

'Well?' she asked first thing. 'How did you explain this to Abigail?'·

He sat down beside her on the couch. 'It didn't come to me until the last second. But I told her I did know about the visit and that I did not let on because it was meant to be a surprise—a Christmas gift.'

'And she believed you?'

'Yes, after Miss Shirls stepped in to confirm it was so.'

'I have a feeling Miss Shirls knows a good bit more about our situation than she lets on.'

He had to catch his breath. Felicia had called it 'our situation.' Spoken so easily, she had no idea what that meant to him. In the past, every problem he had encountered was one he faced alone. Just like that, his wife clicked another number on his heart safe into place. The amazing thing was, not only was she able to do it, but he did not fear the end result as much had he had only days ago.

'I never have been able to keep a secret from Miss Shirls. I wonder if the canny lady has some sixth sense.'

'Well, what do you think of the Penfields?' Felicia asked.

'I cannot say for certain, not yet.' He leaned his head on the back of the couch, closing his eyes. 'Matters are strained between us. Lord Penfield has made no secret of it.'

'Nor have you.'

He felt fingers brush the hair at his temple, the touch so brief and light it might have been a moth fluttering past.

'Here,' she said, tapping on the book. 'I have looked up the meaning of their names. Perhaps it will give us some insight to them.'

He opened his eyes to peer at her. 'You really do believe in names meaning something?'

'Sometimes meanings are spot on. But even when they are not, it is fun to study them.'

'All right, let's try out "Henry."'

She turned a few pages, trailing her slender finger down the list of names.

'Here it is. Henry…"ruler of the home."'

'He is the Earl, so clearly that. What kind of ruler is what I want to know?'

'We will need to learn it for ourselves. But I do get the sense he cares very much for his wife and would go to great ends to make her happy.'

Would the visitors have the same sense about Isaiah? That he cared for Felicia? It was important they did, yet was it not more important for Felicia to know it?

'What about Diana?' he asked. 'Let's look up her name.'

'I already did, before you came in.' Felicia thumbed to the page where the name Diana was at the top of the list. 'It is very interesting. There are a few definitions. One of them is meaningful, but as a contrast. Diana means fertile.'

'Were she that, we would not now be facing this challenge.'

'I feel sad for what she must have gone through all these years, wanting a child and having one denied her month after month. It would break one's heart.'

Would it break hers? By continuing to dodge intimacy, would he doom Felicia to the same fate?

'Do you want a child, Felicia?' He had to know.

'We have discussed this.' She was not looking at him while she spoke, but rather at the names in the book. 'It is a decision for two people to make.'

'Indeed, we have.' And they would discuss it again, but in the moment his attention must be on keeping the child he had. 'So, Henry is the ruler of the home and his wife desperate for a child, be it her own, or mine. I agree the ruler would do whatever it takes to make his wife happy, even if it meant raising the daughter of his brother.'

All of a sudden he felt half-sick. Was Henry Penfield so different a man than his late brother? Would he claim Abigail as his own and then in the end resent her?

'We do not know that he and his brother are anything alike, Isaiah.'

'How did you know what I was wondering?'

'It only made sense you would be.'

Maybe, but she did have a way of seeing inside him whether he wished it or not. Somehow, he found the notion comforting and it was possible that he did wish it.

'But I think he and his brother are not alike. Certainly not in age. Henry Penfield must be much younger than Palmer.'

'Fifteen years, if I remember correctly. I met him once when I was five years old, but I do not recall much about it.'

'As far as I can tell, Lady Penfield is not a bit reserved with her husband. She speaks her mind without fear.'

Unlike his mother, who had been decidedly reserved in the presence of his stepfather. Even as a child he had known something was wrong with that.

'But I think I must speak to Lady Penfield.' Felicia closed the book and patted his hand. 'She needs to know that Abigail is not aware of the reason for their visit. I hope to be able to convince her not to reveal it until—well, there is no until, is there?'

Latching on to her positive attitude, he clung desperately to it, praying she was correct.

After an early dinner, Isaiah and Lord Penfield retired to the library, as men tended to do. Felicia could only wonder how stilted their conversation would be. They had not warmed towards each other during the meal.

'Come, Lady Penfield,' Felicia said. 'Shall we go into the parlour and enjoy the Christmas tree?'

Unlike Isaiah, Felicia was looking forward to spending time with her guest.

'That would be grand. I will soak up every bit of your beautiful tree.' She clapped her hands in clear delight as they turned into the parlour. 'I will admit to shedding a tear for not having put one up this year. No boughs of holly or winter berries either. But Henry and I were so eager to meet Abigail, we made the sacrifice.'

So far she and Isaiah had managed to put off that meeting with one excuse or another, but they could not do it much longer.

No doubt Abigail was as anxious to meet her aunt and uncle as they were to meet her.

'I understand your regret. Christmas really is the best

time of year. Abigail and I went into the woods and cut this tree ourselves while Lord Scarsfeld was on a visit to Windermere. We had such fun with it. I am so happy to be able to share it with you, Lady Penfied.'

'It makes me warm all over just to look at it.' Lady Penfield touched a branch, then looked up, and up, with a smile. 'But, please, you must call me Diana. We are family, after all.'

'I would be delighted to! And you must call me Felicia.'

Good, here was the first step towards forging a friendship—but not one that was for the sake of the battle she and Isaiah were waging. No, indeed, because no matter where Abigail ended up living, it was important to form a genuine kinship with Diana Penfield.

Nothing would be worse for her little sister than to have to go and live with people she and Isaiah were at odds with. The poor child would have her heart ripped down the middle.

'Shall we sit and enjoy the fire?'

'That would be lovely. I do thank you for having dinner served early. Travelling makes Henry hungry. I have never been able to work out why. I wonder, do you have anything to sip while we relax?'

'I was hoping you would suggest it.'

Felicia poured them each a small glass of sherry. They sat in silence for a few moments, sipping while taking in the warmth of the fire, the beauty of the tree.

'I am so anxious to meet Abigail,' Lady Penfield said at last.

'I'm sure she is also anxious to meet you.'

'What is she like? I've wondered and wondered.'

Felicia could do nothing but tell the truth. It could not be long before Abigail came bounding in the room to make her acquaintance, or hobbling as the case was. Lady Penfield would see for herself who the child was whom she hoped to raise.

It would do little good to lie. More than that, it would do a great deal of damage. One could hardly cultivate a friendship born of deception.

'She is quite bright and very inquisitive to go with it. I enjoy her company greatly.'

'You are aware, I'm sure, that Henry and I wish to bring her home with us.'

Felicia could only nod. Discussing this caused a great lump to swell in her throat.

'May I tell you something of myself, Felicia? So perhaps you might understand.'

Again, she could do nothing but nod. She did not want to understand anything except that Abigail would grow up here at Scarsfeld.

'My husband and I have had some disappointments—I have suffered miscarriages. I get to a certain point early on when most ladies would become ill. But then, apparently the pregnancy does not take. Each time it happens my heart breaks a little more and I cry a little longer. After the last time, Henry suggested we bring Abigail to Penfield. I am no longer a young woman, after all, and my chances of conceiving are not—' She swallowed, blinking to hold back the moisture welling in her eyes.

'I'm sorry for your losses, Diana, truly I am.'

And yet, ought the lady's heart be healed at the cost of Abigail's happiness?

The battle for her sister had now become a muddled mess. At first it had seemed so reasonable to do whatever was needed to win the fight. Now that her heart ached for her 'adversary' it was all quite troubling.

If the time ever came when Felicia waited anxiously for her courses to stop, she would be devastated to have them begin again time after time.

Poor Diana. Felicia scarcely knew who to weep for now, Abigail, her brother, the Penfields—or even herself. In the short time she had lived here, she had come to love the child as much as she did the sisters she had been raised with.

'She is full of adventure,' Felicia said past the lump. 'And she has quite a bit to say on every subject you can imagine. Isaiah says she has been stating her opinions from the time she learned to speak.'

'I think she and I will get along famously. I must confess the idea of instructing her to become a lady of society is thrilling.'

This was the time to reveal to Diana what she must. It could not be put off any longer.

'There is something you must know. I hope I can trust you to—well, it must be told regardless.'

'You need not fear, I am good at keeping a confidence.'

'I did not mean to suggest otherwise, but you see, Abigail does not know why you have come. Isaiah told her it was for a Christmas visit only.'

'But surely she must be informed.' Diana's distress was evident. 'It cannot be wise to remain mum on the matter.'

'Perhaps it is not. But you must understand leaving

Scarsfeld will not be what Abigail wants. She and her brother love each other deeply. Since the night she was delivered to Isaiah he has been devoted to her—and she to him, of course. Neither of them had the good fortune to be raised by their mother, but in the end Juliette Penfield did give them to each other.'

'But surely she will want a mother?'

'That is something she can never have—but she will have a sister to stand in a mother's place, or an aunt. If it is you at the end of it, I hope you will come to love her as much as I already do.'

'But of course I will! Never fear on that count.'

Even knowing Diana Penfield for such a short time, she suspected it would be the case.

'She is rather lovable.'

Felicia's next question would put what Diana said to the test. She only hoped Diana would be able to sway her husband's view on the matter.

'I must ask you something, Diana.' It was hard to speak past the cramp in her throat. 'Please do not tell Abigail of your intentions. Wait—get to know her first. If you feel she will not suit for your household, it will spare her grief.'

Diana drank the remaining sherry in her glass in one gulp. Felicia thought it a splendid idea and did the same.

'Yes.' Diana set her glass on the table next to the couch. The glass made a decided clink. 'You make a valid point. Also, it will make the transition easier for her if she knows us first.'

'So you will not tell her yet?'

'I am inclined not to, but there is Lord Penfield to be considered.'

'Do you want to know what I think, my friend?'

'Indeed, I do.'

'I think that Lord Penfield is inclined to think whatever you encourage him to think.'

Diana laughed softly.

'How wise a thing for one so recently wed to understand.'

'I did have the benefit of my mother's example to go by.'

Diana squeezed her hand, smiling. 'I cannot promise anything, but I will see what is to be done in regards to my husband's silence.'

'I meant it, you know, when I called you friend a moment ago. I only hope that, however this turns out, we will remain so.'

'Of course, we must—'

The pleasant exchange was interrupted by the arrival of the men.

It was clear to see by their matching scowls that they had come to no such accord.

Felicia stood, hurrying across the room towards her husband. While she went she gathered her weapons, her arsenal being a smile and a kiss on Isaiah's cheek.

Stiff as starch, he uttered a few words in admiration of the Christmas tree.

And so the skirmish between the Maxwells and the Penfields carried on.

Chapter Eleven

Lord Penfield was as bristly a fellow as Isaiah was. As custom dictated, after dinner he and Penfield spent a few moments in the library, but they were not particularly comfortable.

Such did not seem to be the case with the wives.

After he returned Felicia's brief kiss and then pretended to admire her Christmas tree, she sat back down on the couch beside Lady Penfield.

If he did not know better, he would have thought them great life-long friends.

Listening to them laugh, seeing them smile, he thought women must be very different creatures from men. He did not believe he was mistaken when he heard them already calling each other by their first names. It would be a long time before he and Lord Penfield did the same, if they ever managed it.

'I'll race you down!' Abigail's voice came from the upstairs landing.

'Oh, no, young lady, you will not—' All of a sudden Miss Shirls gasped. The snap of the nanny's starched petticoats rustled with her quick dash down the steps.

Isaiah spun away from his guests, dashed into the hall and caught his sister before she could fall off the end of the banister.

'How many times must I tell you not to do that?' he whispered in order to keep the Penfields from knowing he was overbearing.

He set Abigail on the floor.

'Our girl will do as she pleases, I fear, no matter how many times you caution her.' Miss Shirls bent to smooth a wrinkle from his sister's skirt.

'Are you able to walk?' he asked. 'Otherwise I will carry you.'

'Balance me only. I should like to meet my aunt and uncle while standing. And thank you for letting me stay up to meet them. I would not sleep a wink otherwise.'

It went against everything he thought was best, but he understood her wanting to walk in on her own.

Supporting her under her elbow, he led her into the parlour. It was a relief to see that she hobbled along much better than she had done this morning.

Evidently Miss Shirls did not want to be left out of the introductions. Most servants would remain in the hallway, but he heard her steps firmly walking behind him.

Lady Penfield stood when Abigail inched into the room. Lord Penfield was already standing, but went to the couch to take a place beside his wife.

Isaiah noticed him take her hand, holding it unseen within the folds of her skirt.

It was clear that this meeting meant very much to both of them. As much as he wished to believe they were a selfish pair, coveting what was not theirs, he could not help but wonder if they were also nervous.

This was the last thing he wanted to wonder because he did not wish to witness vulnerability and longing in the couple. All he wanted was for the two of them to leave Scarsfeld without Abigail and never come back.

'Good evening, dear girl!' Lady Penfield hurried forward, her hands clasped at her middle. Isaiah had the sense that she wanted to go down on her knees and embrace Abigail. 'What a pleasure it is to meet you at last.'

Balancing on his arm, his sister presented a small curtsy.

'Thank you, Aunt, it is a pleasure to meet you, too.'

'My lady,' Miss Shirls said with her own slight dip. 'Welcome to Scarsfeld.'

One thing that Isaiah and the nanny had in common was the inability to hide a displeased emotion. It might be why they got on so easily together.

But he got along with his wife, too, and she was always smiling. Even in this critical moment when one of the Penfields might blurt out their intention to steal his sister away from home, Felicia was nothing if not poised.

What he should do was strive to be more like her.

'Oh, my goodness!' Lady Penfield exclaimed, noticing the bandages wrapped around Abigail's ankle. 'You have been injured.'

His sister lifted her hem, turned her foot this way and that. 'It was all in the name of fun so it is not as horrid as it seems.'

'I'm sure it will not hamper your visit with your niece in any way, Lady Penfield,' he admitted.

Calling this a visit was not what it was. To his way of thinking, it was more of an abduction. One of the Penfields was surely about to point it out at any second.

Lord Penfield stepped forward, lifted Abigail's chin and peered into her eyes.

'I assume, young lady that you know why my wife and I have come?'

Isaiah opened his mouth, having no idea what words were going to burst out, only that they would not be pleasant.

'Oh, Henry…' Lady Penfield neatly stepped between her husband and Abigail, breaking the contact of his hand on her chin. 'The whole household knows that we have come for a visit. To spend Christmas with our family and get to know them all.'

'I, for one, believe there is no better way to spend Christmas,' Felicia added, slipping her arm about the Countess's waist and giving her a hug.

There was more happening here than met the eye.

'But should the child not—' Lord Penfield looked perplexed.

That was something he and his opponent had in common: perplexity.

'Get to know us?' Lady Penfield arched a brow at her husband. 'And we get to know her? This will be the happiest Christmas we have spent in a very long time, do you not agree?'

He raised one brow back at her. 'Oh, yes, indeed. I have no doubt of it.'

'Yes, quite so. Being stranded at the estate because of the storm, we could not ask for a better chance to become acquainted,' the countess said.

Isaiah looked at Felicia, who was smiling brightly at Lady Penfield.

Hmm... Things were afoot that mere males had no idea of.

Thankfully, for the moment at least, it appeared that Abigail would not know how her future hung in the balance.

The next afternoon Abigail decided it would be grand fun for all of them to decorate the pine cones and twigs that Felicia had gathered.

Isaiah looked up from his place at the long table where they were seated.

Lord Penfield twisted a twig in his fingers, staring at it in bewilderment.

Glancing up at Isaiah, he shrugged. What was he to do with the thing? his expression asked. At least Isaiah and the Earl were allies in something.

Abigail rolled a spool of ribbon towards them. It was red and green plaid, edged in some fragile-looking white lace.

'Simply wrap the ribbon around however you like.' She held up the one she was working on. 'Like this.'

Penfield cut a length of ribbon and draped it over the top of the cone. It resembled a limp noodle.

'Really, dear, it is not so difficult. Just wrap the ribbon around and tie it in a bow.'

'Ever tie a bow, Scarsfeld?' he asked while fumbling with the ribbon.

'Only knots in rope.' He snipped a length of ribbon longer than the one Penfield had cut. It tangled in his fingers when he tried to copy what the ladies were doing. 'I'll just watch and see how you do it.'

There was an undercurrent of competition going on between them and, oddly, it felt—fun. It took him aback because he had not expected any sort of camaraderie with this man.

When he thought about it, he realised his animosity towards the Earl was not only to do with Abigail. Indeed, he had always harboured an uncomfortable feeling towards the fellow. He did not know this for certain, but it was likely that Lord Penfield had known his mother. While Isaiah had been weeping his seven-year-old eyes dry, was Penfield basking in Mama's love?

That was an unfair way to think. It would hardly be his fault if Isaiah's mother had showed Penfield favour as a young man.

'Between you and me,' Isaiah said softly in hopes that the women would not hear, 'your bow is sensible and to the point.'

'Perhaps, but by its very nature a bow goes against sensibility. It will secure nothing heavier than a feather, I fear.'

'That is not our concern. It is for us to simply get the ribbons on in a fluffy way.'

'Yours is sagging.'

All of a sudden Isaiah wanted to smile. He could not possibly, though. He would do well to remember the man was a foe and not a friend. To make him one would be a betrayal of his sister.

Yet, watching his wife laugh with Lady Penfield, he had to wonder. Clearly she had no problem with the divide between friend and foe.

Had she ever met anyone she considered a foe? It might account for her cheerful attitude towards life if that were the case.

Looking at her now, ruffling Abigail's hair, advising Lady Penfield on which shade of red lace to use, he could only admit he was grateful she was this way.

What if life could always be lived how it was at this moment? With family gathered about a table and the only storm the one now beating the walls of the mansion.

What if—never mind. There was a storm inside this house as well as outside. In the end it, hearts would be ravaged, not bonded.

After tea, Felicia carried an armload of decorated pine cones into the hall. She set them on the floor while the men carried the rest into the parlour.

'This will be the most festive our house has ever been!' Abigail declared cheerfully, limping past and hugging a large spool of ribbon to her chest.

'Will it?' Lady Penfield asked, following behind with more ribbon.

Felicia did not miss the slight frown creasing her brow.

'Yes, but because you are here.'

Lady Penfield's frown dissolved into a smile. She tugged the bow in Abigail's hair. 'And we are so pleased to be, my dear.'

'Do you think our husbands have made a bit of peace with each other?' Felicia asked, feeling a bit shaken watching a bond begin to form between aunt and niece.

Lady Penfield tapped her chin, watching the men's

efforts to hang a ribbon from a rafter. 'They could not help but feel each other's misery during the decorating. So perhaps, yes, they have—in as much as they can.'

'Let us hope. It does a family no good at all to be at odds with one another,' Felicia whispered out of Abigail's hearing.

Or to fear growing bonds.

'I like feeling that we are family,' Felicia whispered again even more softly. 'I must thank you for encouraging Lord Penfield to keep his silence. Whoever wins this tug of war over Abigail, we do not want her torn up over it.'

'Of course not. Love does not behave that way. I think that we can agree any decision which is made must be done with love.'

'I never expected to like you so quickly and so well, Diana.'

'And I never expected to be welcomed into your home so genuinely.'

Inside the parlour everything was a bustle with Abigail directing her brother and her uncle on where to hang the decorations.

Mr Phillips came in with a ladder and stayed to lend a hand with the hanging.

Eloise wandered in. Within a moment Lord Penfield began to sneeze so she was shooed from the room. Wasn't it interesting that a cat could actually look affronted?

It took a long while to finish. It was not until the time to dress for dinner that the last pine cone glittered from its spot on the mantelpiece.

Glancing about, Felicia had to catch her breath. She stood in a place of enchantment, of wonder which would thrill the most sober of hearts.

Everyone retired to their rooms, but Felicia lingered, a riot of leftover ribbon curling about her skirt.

What a beautiful afternoon it had been. One could nearly forget the heartache that was coming to sadden them all.

She no longer believed that the Penfields would be able to take Abigail away from her home and not suffer remorse for it.

Closing her eyes, she let the scent of the Christmas tree fill her up. Lovely memories of the past with her family blended in her heart with the ones she was making today.

What would life be without Christmas? So much love was expressed at this time of year.

A flutter tickled her neck. Opening her eyes, she found a wide ribbon settling in place across her shoulders.

'You need a lesson in colour co-ordination, Isaiah. This blue plaid does not suit my gown.'

Wrapping the ends of the ribbon in his fists, he drew her towards him.

'What are you doing?'

'What do you think I am doing?'

Evidently he meant to kiss her. Her knees would not feel like mush and her heart would not be beating triple time if it were not true.

'My question is, why are you doing it? Everyone has gone upstairs so we need not put on a show.'

'Are you really who you seem to be, Felicia?' He tied the ribbon in a bow, of sorts, across her bosom.

'I imagine I am. You are the one who is a chameleon.'

'Are you sorry to have married such a crusty fellow?' he asked while fingering the loops of the bow and drawing her closer.

'Crusty?' Lightly, hesitantly, she touched his vest, felt his heart thumping hard under her fingertips. 'You are wounded, Isaiah. You are not crusty in here.'

'Abigail says I am.' Closer now, his breath warmed her cheeks.

'Well, she is only eight and must be excused for it.' Felicia held his gaze because for once his heart seemed open and so very vulnerable. She could all but hear his thoughts.

'I need to know—do you regret our marriage? If you had it to do over again, would you choose a love match instead of what I offer you?'

She touched his lips, thinking how wonderful it would be if he did kiss her. 'I am not convinced that I have not made a love match.'

'What are you saying, Felicia?' Even her fingers thrilled to the touch of his lips.

'I am saying you ought to give me this kiss so that I might learn the truth of the matter.'

'You undo me.' His voice was raspy and, she thought, expressed fear of what she just revealed.

Ah, but then his kiss fell upon her, possessive and capitulating all in one hot, breathless moment.

She knew the truth, as unlikely as that truth was. In spite of everything, she had made a love match.

When the kiss finally ended, she spun away, clutched the bow to her heart and dashed out of the parlour.

The very last thing she wanted was for him to respond to what she'd admitted.

He was not ready yet. She only prayed that one day he would be.

The truth of the matter was that he had kissed Felicia, yet again. He not could say he regretted doing it, but he could not say acting upon the impulse had not left him sleepless—yet again.

That must mean something, other than he would be tired in the morning.

But tonight's restlessness was different.

Words had been spoken which did not fit in with what he had first expected of this marriage. In the beginning he had been fool enough to imagine any woman would be satisfied with what he offered, a title and his beautiful estate.

His wife was not merely any woman. She was exceptional—she was relentless and he feared she would not be satisfied until she had all of him.

But did he fear it, really?

Sentiments had been shared which rocked his core, shook his heart. Was it possible that his shaking foundation might have as much to do with anticipation as dread?

He was the one to have brought up the subject of a love match. Her response was not at all what he had expected to hear.

No. In asking he sought an affirmation, a reassurance that she would be content even if she did not have one.

It nearly laid him out when she suggested that she might have found it.

And then she had fled, the ends of the ribbon that did not match her gown flapping like blue wings in her wake.

He had not thought before speaking, but only blurted out what was on his mind.

The shock of it was that it *was* on his mind. Why was it on his mind?

Had he, too, made a love match? If he had, did he dare to accept it?

If he did accept it, it would mean Felicia was well secured in his heart. It would mean losing her, for any reason, was something he could not endure.

To say he was troubled did not begin to describe the state he was in, which was why he was on his way to the library in the wee hours. He had never spent time wandering about his house late at night until Felicia came to him.

The library door was closed, but light seeped out from under it, casting a warm glow on the hallway floor.

He nearly turned away to seek another place to brood. He did not want to discuss matters of the heart—not yet. He needed time to think, to search his soul and discover what he really wanted from her.

Still, he would not flee his own library.

He opened the door, stepping boldly inside.

It was hard to know if he was relieved or disappointed that it was Penfield sitting in the chair in front of the fire and not Felicia.

One thing for sure, he would enjoy his wife's company more than he would his rival's.

Yet he did have it in his heart to speak to the man. There might not be a better opportunity.

'Good evening, Scarsfeld, or rather later than that, isn't it?'

'I've lost track. It might be early morning.'

'Perhaps you are losing sleep because of a woman, just as I am?'

'In fact, yes. Three of them.' Tonight his mother was on his mind along with Felicia and Abigail.

'You have my condolences.'

Settling in the other chair, Isaiah stretched his feet towards the flames.

'It is hard to imagine this storm could get any worse,' Isaiah muttered. Only he knew he had not referred to the weather, but to the storm whooshing about the walls of his own home.

'And here you are stuck with guests you must wish to be rid of.'

It was not they as much as what they threatened, he did have to admit that much truth. Lady Penfield was a goodhearted woman and he thought she would not love her husband unless he had a few redeeming virtues.

'I assume you had my sister's presumed best interests in mind when you decided she should come to live with you.'

'We can offer her many things in London.'

'It was my mother's wish that I raise Abigail. I have never regretted a moment of it.'

'My wife and I have many regrets.' Lord Penfield drummed his fingers on the arm of his chair. 'We desire a child, you will know that, I think. I fear it is the one thing I am unable to give her. Loving her so much,

I would do anything to make her happy. Surely you understand what I feel?'

Lord Penfield gave him a look that clearly accused his presumed marriage of convenience as one lacking in affection.

'I would do anything to make my sister happy.' It was not the answer Penfield was seeking, but the only one he was going to get.

'I do not doubt that. You may rest assured that Lady Penfield and I will do no less for her.'

Penfield became quiet for a time, looking down his long nose at the flames snapping in the fireplace.

'There is something I can put your mind to rest about.' When he glanced over at Isaiah, he saw sincerity reflected in the man's expression. 'I am nothing like my brother was.'

No, he would not be. Palmer Penfield had wanted nothing to do with another man's child. Henry Penfield clearly wanted everything to do with his brother's child.

Arguing over who had rights to Abigail would be futile right now so Isaiah turned his mind to the other matter pressing upon him.

'Did you know my mother?'

Even under the beak Isaiah saw a genuine smile.

'Of course. Before I left for Oxford I lived at Penfield. What would you like to know?'

Why did she stop loving me? Did you replace me in her heart? Why did she never come back home?

'Was she happy?' He wondered that, too. Was she content after she left him behind?

'No one was happy living with my brother. Especially not your mother. She tried her best to please him, but he was a man who could not be pleased. Even if she had given him a dozen heirs, he would not have been satisfied. Do you want to know the truth, Isaiah? It will not be pleasant to hear.'

'I do not, but I think I must.'

'Your mother was under my brother's control—what she said, who she met—she did nothing without his approval and he approved of very little.'

'Did he forbid her to come and see me?'

'He did and I watched it break her. I imagine you will be wondering, did I take your place?'

He nodded because his throat closed so tightly he thought he might strangle.

'I tried to. I hoped it might help her, you understand. But I think I only reminded her of what she had lost in you. She could not speak of you, my brother did not allow it. He hoped she would forget you eventually. When I made my escape to college, she was deep in melancholy. I'm sorry. I wish I could have done something but—a mother's love—she needed you and no other.'

Isaiah sat silently, his resentment for his stepfather growing more bitter than ever.

'In the end there is Abigail,' Lord Penfield muttered. 'The former Earl did one thing right.'

Yes, there was Abigail. How ironic was it that the man who had taken the love of his mother from him had given it back in the form of his sister.

'You will think me uncharitable to say so, but I've often thought it was good that he died before he knew he had fathered a girl and not his heir.'

'Do you think he would have mistreated his own

child?' The thought of anyone being unkind to his sister blurred his vision in a red haze.

'He mistreated his wife, so, yes, I do. Women were of no value to him.'

Isaiah curled his fists, digging his fingernails into his palms. All this time he had resented what his mother had done to him when all along she'd had no choice because of what had been done to her. She was the late Earl's victim as every bit as much as he had been.

The rub of it was, he had been so consumed with his own unhappiness that he had never considered that to be the case. He must have grunted or growled, because Penfield slid his glance sideways.

'I would have done something if I could have. Please do not think I would not. My brother kept me away much of the time in order to prevent it.'

'I believe you are telling me the truth.' Isaiah forced his hands to press flat on the chair arms. 'I will also be truthful with you, Penfield.'

'If you must.' The comment was softened by his smile.

'I did not want you to come here. I bore you hostile feelings—even as far as thinking of you as my foe. I confess, I no longer think that.'

'What man would not feel the same?' Lord Penfield asked.

'Not many I know of. But our wives—have you noticed how they became fast friends from the moment they met?'

'Indeed. They deal with the issue between us far better than we do.'

'I will strive to follow their example,' Isaiah promised. 'But you might know some people believe me to be less than cheerful.'

'Reputations do not necessarily reflect the truth. I would know this since I have struggled with people seeing my brother in me.'

'I do not see him,' Isaiah admitted because the truth was the truth.

And yet, it changed little. Abigail lay between them as solid as a wedge lodged in a log.

Chapter Twelve

In Felicia's opinion, Lord Penfield was the perfect choice to read from Charles Dickens's *A Christmas Carol*.

Somehow the shape of his nose alone added to the drama of the Christmas ghost story. Added to that the storm scratching at the windows, moaning and howling to get in… Well, a delicious shiver prickled up her back.

Back at Cliverton House, Christmas could not fully arrive until the book was finished, which always happened on Christmas Eve.

With three days until then, the timing was perfect.

Abigail sat on the floor in front of the hearth. It was odd to see her without Eloise contentedly purring in her lap, but Lord Penfield would never have made it through the story had she been. The poor man burst into sneezing fits whenever the cat was nearby.

Lord Penfield turned his chair so that everyone could see and hear him clearly.

"'Stave One: Marley's Ghost,'" he read, his brows shooting up and his voice going deep, as if the said ghost might suddenly drift into the parlour, his white robes aflutter or perhaps even followed by Scrooge, his chains rattling. "'Marley was dead to begin with. There was no doubt whatever about that.'"

Felicia closed her eyes to better allow the author's words to come to life in her mind.

A few days ago she would not have thought the five of them could be gathered so happily. Indeed, even yesterday there had been an air of wariness between Isaiah and Lord Penfield. While there was still a sense of stress between them, she no longer feared they would go for each other's throats.

"'Old Marley was as dead as a doornail.'" Lord Penfield nodded while he read. 'Mind, I don't mean to say that I know, of my own knowledge, what there is particularly dead about a doornail.'

Abigail began to giggle.

'Really, my dear.' Lady Penfield smiled brightly at her husband. 'No one reads this story as well as you do! Had you not been born to a title you might have been a great success on stage.'

'I would run to see your performances, Uncle!' Abigail's delight at having her aunt and uncle here to share Christmas was evident in her smile, in the happy sparkle in her eyes.

Of course, if she knew the true reason for their 'visit' she might feel quite differently. For all that Lord and Lady Penfield were not the despicable and selfish relatives both she and Isaiah had first believed them to be, they were still a threat to Abigail's well-being.

It made matters all the harder because they were

well intentioned. Felicia truly felt great sorrow for their plight.

'At Penfield I read the story every year to the servants' children.'

'It is the best time,' Lady Penfield added. 'When the story is finished we give gifts to the children and everyone eats jam tarts.'

'What a grand time!' Abigail's grin with her missing tooth was one of the most endearing things Felicia had ever seen. She felt all warm inside just looking at it. 'Until this year it's been only me and Isaiah to give out Christmas treats.'

'I wonder if you would like to come back to London with us?' Lord Penfield asked.

It was as if a shroud soaked in icy water had been cast over the adults. Lord Penfield blinked at his wife's frown, realising he had spoken out of turn, and his large Adam's apple bobbed up and down.

'For a visit, I mean.'

'May we, Isaiah? I would love to visit London.'

Lord Penfield cleared his throat and pressed on with the story. '"Scrooge knew he was dead. Of course he did."'

Lady Penfield nodded once quite sharply.

With any luck Abigail had not noticed the sudden tension between the adults. No one in this room wished her to feel frightened for her future.

Felicia's joy in hearing the story was dimmed. She knew very well that Lord Penfield had not been suggesting a visit. What she wanted to do was weep but, of course, Abigail would wonder why she was.

So she sat, hands folded on her lap while presenting a smile her heart did not feel.

At last Lord Penfield said, '"…went straight to bed without undressing, and fell asleep upon the instant."' Then he closed the book.

Abigail hopped up. 'Perhaps Cook has left us tarts in the kitchen!'

One by one they trailed behind her. Felicia hoped there were tarts. Everyone could use a dash of sugar in the here and now.

Isaiah walked up the stairs beside Felicia, shoulders nearly touching while they made their way towards their chambers.

After the turn the evening had taken, he was beyond grateful to have her beside him.

'What do you think?' he asked. 'Are they going to tell her?'

'Lord Penfield nearly slipped up,' she said. He wished her sigh did not sound so resigned. A response more like a battle cry would have made him feel better. 'I thought Diana had managed to convince him to wait until after Christmas. I do not think he meant to say what he did. It's only that the evening was so pleasant… All of us gathered for the story like a proper, affectionate family. Honestly, Isaiah, I think he was simply speaking from his heart. I do think they care for her very much.'

Standing in the hallway between his suite of rooms and hers, he could not help himself and let out a resigned sigh. He shook his head, feeling confused and defeated.

'Do you think it is unfair of me to keep her from

them, Felicia?' He looked at the rug while he spoke because he was cut up by what he was about to say. 'I wonder if she would be happier in London. They can give her social benefits that I cannot.'

He felt her fingers in his hair, gently stroking a trail from his temple to the curve of his ear, as she had a way of doing. The gesture was amazingly comforting.

No one had comforted him this way since he was a very small child. How had he managed all these years without Felicia?

'She is only eight years old. Perhaps ten years from now that will be a boon to her, but not yet. She belongs here with you.'

'But I only wonder if she ought to be able to choose.'

'If it came to that, she would choose you, never fear it.'

He turned his face, kissing her palm.

'May I come in?' he asked with a nod at her side of the hallway.

It had been a night for ghosts, it was time to put one of them to rest.

'I would enjoy your company. This is not a time for being alone,' she said while opening the door.

He followed her inside, prepared for the rush of pain that always came from entering this chamber.

The space was warm from the small fire snapping and popping in the hearth. Only one lamp was lit so everything was cheerfully aglow in amber light.

He stood still, glancing at dim corners while Felicia sat down at her dressing table and began to take the pins out of her hair.

For once, his mother did not come to him joyful and

laughing, nor did she stare at him with vacant eyes. In fact, she did not come to him at all.

Pain did not rip his heart apart even though it was no longer as dead as Mr Dicken's doornail.

'It is no longer snowing, thank the good Lord.' She glanced back at him with a smile. 'I imagine you never thought to hear me say that.'

He walked across the room, holding her gaze as if it were a lifeline and he a sinking man.

But he was not sinking, except to his knees beside Felicia's chair.

'I think—well, there is something I wish to point out.' He caught a lock of red hair as it tumbled free of its pin, then twined it between his fingers. The thought coming to his mind was that her hair was a Christmas ribbon and she the gift he would unwrap.

'It will be less tangled after I brush it.' Her cheeks flashed a beguiling shade of pink.

She must know he was not speaking of untidy locks.

'Yes—and I will be less tangled once I—' Was he really going to say this out loud? Perhaps it would be wiser not to, but more than that, he would be a huge fool not to say it. 'It is my belief that there cannot be a love match when there is only one involved in it. A match requires two, don't you think?'

'There are unrequited loves in which—'

'Still, not a match.'

Before she could try to convince him of her point he kissed her. He gently tugged her hair with one hand while sliding her off the chair, his arm firmly around her waist.

He set her on the floor, his thighs braced on either side of her.

'Felicia,' he whispered across her cheek. 'I am the other side of your love match.'

What?

Felicia slid away, but not so very far that she could not slide back in a hurry.

Surely she must have misheard? Or, if she had not, perhaps he had declared it on a whim and would now take back those very precious words.

'I beg your pardon?' If he *did* mean what he said, her response was the least romantic in the history of declarations of love.

His smile was the best and brightest she had ever seen. It turned her into a puddle—not mud, but chocolate—rich, smooth and simmering.

'No, I beg yours.'

Well, then! She slid back to him.

He gathered her into the circle of his arms. Strong muscles hugged her so solidly and yet at the same time so tenderly that she felt as if nothing could ever go wrong again. Or if it did she need never face it alone.

'It is a wonder you did not run for home on our wedding day. I beg your pardon for doing it all so poorly... I truly regret I was so...'

He seemed to have trouble coming up with a suitable word.

'Overwhelmed?' she suggested. 'We were strangers committing our lives to each other. Both of us were rather staggered with what we were about to do. One thing about it, Isaiah, I do not regret that there was no music. Otherwise you would not have sung me down the stairs. I think I would follow your voice anywhere, it touches me so.'

'Everything about you touches me. From the very start you have gone straight to my heart. It only took me a while to trust it.'

'And no wonder. You suffered what no child ever should have done.'

Had they not married to try to prevent such a thing happening to Abigail?

Of course the silver linings of their situation were beginning to gleam. Was she not sitting on the floor with this man, nearly ready to make her way from here to the bed?

The great miracle of love was that it was sometimes born of pain. This was a profound thought that only just this moment had occurred to her.

'But love finds a way,' he whispered as if he had made the discovery in the same instant she did.

What were the odds that they would think the same thing at the same time? Very slim—unless the spirit of love explained it to them, both in the same thought.

No one could know that for certain, but it seemed a lovely and reasonable way to account for it.

'Felicia Merry Penneyjons, I love you. Will you marry me—continue to, I mean?'

'Isaiah Elphalet Maxwell, you know very well I will. And I will love you "in the city of gold, my dearest, dearest heart."' She did not sing that last for fear of ruining the moment.

'And I,' he murmured, his voice going low and husky—a sound which thrilled nerves she had never expected to be thrilled, 'will love you in that bed.'

He stood, giving her a hand up.

For the longest time they simply looked at each other, as if the moment was enchanted and they were loath to leave it.

But in Felicia's opinion, a moment even more magical awaited.

'I'll race you to it!'

When she made a dash for the bed she heard him laughing.

Nothing that happened under those covers would be more magical than that.

Isaiah Maxwell was a married man.

Not that he hadn't been one all along, but now he felt like one.

Isaiah Maxwell was also a happy man—a cheerful man.

If anyone could see him now sitting at his desk in the library, staring at the ledgers and grinning, they would not know who he was.

No more than he knew who he was. How could he have guessed that when Felicia spun the final number on the lock of his safe, light would come spilling out? That it would flash into every dark corner and send darkness packing?

He tapped his finger on the page, not really seeing what it said. It was a wonder that he saw anything but the love glowing in his wife's eyes when he had made love to her—until the early hours of dawn.

How many more hours until he could hunt her down, sneak away from company and fall upon the bed with her? Find joy in a place where there had been only pain.

Felicia had been quite right in her belief that good memories could vanquish bad ones. Until last night he had not been fully convinced.

Oh, but he was now. Sitting here waiting for the house to quiet down for the night—he was completely, irrevocably persuaded.

A movement in the doorway caught his eye.

'Would you like some company?' Leaning against the door frame, Felicia shot him a wink.

Excellent! He would not have to waste time finding her. Posed as she was, he thought she looked like— there were too many wonderful things she looked like for him to pick one.

'You were already keeping me company.' He tapped his heart to show her where. 'What is everyone else up to?'

'Our guests have retired early.' She winked and he knew the gesture had something to do with romance. What he did not know was whose romance it was. Lord and Lady Penfield's? Or had they sensed the change in him and Felicia today and gone upstairs to give them a bit of privacy?

Which he intended to take full advantage of.

'Close the door behind you, Felicia.'

The smile she gave him while she leaned into it, fingers splayed against the wood, was one he would store in his memory for ever. Keep it as a treasure to look at whenever he wanted to.

All of a sudden Felicia lurched forward.

Miss Shirls burst into the library.

'Are we to make a trip to London? Abigail is all abuzz over it.'

'Where is my sister, Miss Shirls?'

'Tucked into her bed and reading a good-night story to her cat.'

'Abigail is mistaken. We are not going to London.' Dash it, he did not want to think of going anywhere but upstairs with his bride.

'That is good news. But she is quite certain of it and I, for one, think something is afoot. I have felt it in my bones since the moment Lord and Lady Penfield marched grandly in our front door.'

'You should tell her, Isaiah. Abigail is as dear to Miss Shirls as she is to us—her employment is—'

'They have come to take her away!' The governess slammed her hands on her hips. 'I know it without you having to speak the words.'

It was a lucky thing his sister was upstairs. The governess was not expressing her displeasure quietly.

'It is not for certain they will. But, yes, Miss Shirls, it was their intention to take her back to London with them.'

'They will not take her from me, I can tell you that! She has been my poppet since she was a few days old and that she will remain, even if I have to move to London with her. And believe me, Miss Eloise will not be going to London. Not with His Lordship sneezing his nose off whenever she is within sight.'

'Lord and Lady Penfield are not heartless,' Felicia said, 'They…'

Her voice faded, then she gasped.

Eloise pattered into the room—followed directly by Abigail.

'You promised!' Tears dripped down the child's pale

face. Her bottom lip trembled. 'Isaiah, you promised I would not have to go anywhere I do not wish to.'

'Are you certain you do not wish to?' Clearly she did not, but the question needed asking. 'Your aunt and uncle can give you many advantages.'

'I will not go! No one can make me!' She dashed out of the room. 'Eloise and I will run away to live with the circus!' her voice sobbed from the hallway.

She must think he had betrayed her. What she said cut him to the quick. It felt as though he had done so even though he had fought to prevent this moment.

Still, he had kept her ignorant of what was going on. Yet he had been correct to do so. Anyone young enough to threaten to run off with the circus was too young to be told the truth.

Her tears cut his heart, filling him with guilt whether or not it was warranted. With her emotions undone, would she run outdoors in search of the circus? But, no, she was wise enough not to. When she had wandered off as a baby she had not understood what could happen.

'She does not mean it.' Felicia leaned her head on his shoulder, watching the cat rub her tail on the doorway going out.

'Children do say such things without meaning them,' Miss Shirls declared, then hurried after Abigail.

He thought the same. Her disappearance was not a problem he would need to deal with. Addressing her fear of being taken away was.

'We will work a way out of this,' Felicia whispered. 'Do not worry, Isaiah. Between us, we will.'

For all that it felt as though life had come crashing

down upon him, it was not only him. His wife stood shoulder to shoulder with him.

Because she did, his heart went on beating. They would find a way out of the nightmare.

'I cannot find her!'

Felicia looked past Isaiah's shoulder at Miss Shirls standing in the hallway outside her bedchamber. A moment earlier her loud rap on the door had jarred them from a lovely moment. From bliss to dread in the space of a heartbeat.

'What do you mean?'

'Gone! I do not know where she is.'

'Where have you looked?' Isaiah grabbed his robe while he spoke.

'I came here straight away when she was not in bed where I left her.'

'What about Eloise?' Felicia asked, watching her husband stomp into his slippers. 'The cat will likely be where Abigail is.'

'I have not seen her, either.'

'Alert the household, even those who have retired for the evening. We will search the house.'

'What if she has gone out?'

Already in the hallway, he paused to say, 'She won't have. Even if she did not have a care for her own safety, she would for her cat.'

And then he was off on a run, shouting his sister's name.

Within seconds she heard other voices calling.

A dozen or more people would be searching inside,

but someone needed to make absolutely certain she had not gone out.

Hurriedly, Felicia put her coat on over her night-gown. She stepped into her boots without a thought for stockings.

There was but one thing on her mind: finding her little sister.

Dashing out of the room, then down the steps, she hurried past the Penfields standing in the hall. Lady Penfield was crying while Lord Penfield patted her back.

'Check the cupboards!' she called.

It would help them to be doing something useful. Give an outlet for the fear. And perhaps Abigail was hiding in a cupboard.

Felicia rushed to the conservatory. It was where she, herself would hide if she needed to. There were shrubs and trees to duck behind. It was also a likely place to sneak outside.

'Abigail?' she called, softly. Perhaps if she sounded calm her sister would emerge from hiding.

Nothing. Not even a rustle of fabric gave answer.

Felicia hurried to the set of doors. They were closed, but something caught her eye on the stone floor. She bent to touch it, then recoiled from the icy drops of water.

Someone had opened the door and not so long ago.

Could Abigail have heard everyone calling for her and run outside, thinking she might be disciplined for causing such a stir?

It would be sensible to find Isaiah and show him

what she had discovered. Two would be able to search outside better than only one.

As logical as that seemed, it would take too long. If Abigail *had* gone out, there was no time to be spared.

She stared hard out of the window, praying Abigail had not ventured beyond the terrace.

Even though it was not snowing, wind blew every which way. It disturbed the surface of the powdery snow, making it look something like fog, shifting this way one moment and that the next.

She stepped outside.

'Abigail!' Her shout was caught away as if it had never been.

Chapter Thirteen

Hearing a shout, Isaiah bolted up from looking under a bed in a seldom-used guest room.

'We've found her!'

The cry came from the floor below and he could not tell who it was who'd made the discovery.

He took the stairs down in three, sliding leaps.

People from all over the house came running to the hall.

His sister stood surrounded by her searchers, looking small and distraught.

'We found her in the pantry in the company of her cat,' Lord Penfield stated, looking troubled rather than relieved.

But he would be. The Earl must understand that she had hidden away because of him and his wife—or what they wished of her.

If anything could make them reconsider, surely it was this. Nothing Abigail said would be more convincing than what she had done.

Which was to scare the life out of them all. As much as he did not wish to address it, he must.

'Come with me, Abigail.'

Just because he needed to address her behaviour, he did not need to do it in front of everyone. He held his hand out to her and she took it.

Going into the parlour, he closed the door.

He sat in a chair. She climbed on to his lap and curled into a small, sad heap. She had grown a bit too big to be doing it, but she did fit and so he wrapped her up.

'I am sorry I did not tell you why the Penfields came. I hoped they would see how happy you were living here with me and give up the idea.'

'Well…' she smeared the tears on her cheek with the back of her hand '… I like them very much. But I love you and Felicia. They cannot force me, can they?'

'I imagine they could. Your uncle outranks me socially. If it went to court, he would probably win. It is not what you want to hear, I know. But I do not think it will come to it. You know by now they are decent people. Your uncle only wants to make your aunt happy and since she seems not to be able to have a child of their own—'

'They think I might be their child! But I am eight years old and halfway done with being one already.'

'Abigail, you must promise that no matter what happens, you will not hide from us again. The whole household was turned out of their beds to search for you.'

'I'm sorry, Isaiah. I ought to have thought first.'

'I'm only glad you knew not to go outside to find a travelling circus.'

'Even I know how dangerous it is out there.'

'Now you must apologise to everyone.'

'I suppose I do owe them that.'

He lifted her off his lap. She followed him back to the hall.

A few people frowned at her while she gave her regrets, but not many. Everyone just seemed relieved that she was safely found.

Isaiah looked around. Where was Felicia? Perhaps she was in the attic, still searching, but a stir had been created when his sister was found. She ought to be here.

'Where is Lady Scarsfeld?' he asked, cutting off Abigail's speech of contrition only halfway finished. 'Has anyone seen her?'

Heads shook as everyone glanced around as if puzzled to find she was not among them.

'The last I noticed she was going in the direction of the conservatory,' offered Mrs Muldoon. 'But that was some time ago.'

Rushing across the conservatory, Isaiah heard footsteps thumping behind him.

'Surely she would not have gone out!' Lord Penfield caught up to him, breathing heavily from the run.

'She would if she thought Abigail went that way.'

'But—'

'The door is not properly shut, Penfield. She has gone out.'

'Then we shall, too.'

The Earl nearly beat him on to the terrace.

'You look near the lake. I'll search the front road.'

Near the road where years before he had hunted for his mother on a night similar to this one, searched in vain until he was a broken child, both in heart and body.

This search would not be in vain. He would not return to the house without his wife. Not even if he froze where he stood, he would not stop searching.

He would not huddle under the Christmas tree and weep as he had then. Forcefully, he shook the memory off. Back then, his mother had not been there to find.

Right now, Felicia was out there waiting for him to bring her home.

He did not think she was still looking for Abigail. If she were, he would see her, hear her voice.

Unless she was near the lake. But so far Lord Penfield had not called out to alert him she had been found.

High stepping in order to clear his feet of the deep snow, he plodded to the front of the house.

If Felicia had fallen, she would be covered by the icy powder blowing across the ground.

What if he had walked past her unknowing? Even though she could not have gone far, she might freeze before he found her.

He shouted…shouted again. The only answer was Felicia's name distantly echoed by Lord Penfield.

Wind buffeted him, scratching bare branches together, which gave them the effect of laughing at him, the same as they had done all those years ago.

Once again—this was now, not then. Felicia had not ridden off in a carriage, she was somewhere out here waiting, urgently needing him to find her.

Stare as he might, he could not see her. It could only mean the thing he dreaded.

She had fallen.

He had to fight the panic creeping into his brain, turning his stomach inside out and making him ineffective.

Branches! How many times had he warned his sister not to play under trees when the wind was blowing?

But there were hundreds of trees! If she had been hit by a limb, it would probably have happened near the road since that was where Felicia would have very probably been searching.

The crackle of splintering wood came to him, sharp in contrast to the moan of wind.

Spinning about, he spotted a limb crashing on the ground.

There were branches missing above the one that had fallen.

Knees pumping high, he raced for the spot where the limb lay half buried in snow.

There! The streak of red was nearly covered by drifting snow. Had he been scanning the area more quickly he would have missed it.

Within one long heartbeat he was kneeling beside Felicia. He lifted her out of the icy blanket.

A movement at the front door caught his eye.

'Mr Phillips!' he shouted. 'Over here!'

Lord Penfield must have heard, too, because Isaiah caught his shout of 'huzzah' from down by the lake.

The butler was beside him in only a few moments even with the snow dragging his steps.

'Praise the Good Lord you have found the mistress!' He helped Isaiah carry her. 'That is a nasty-looking gash on her head. Shall I go to the village and fetch the doctor?'

'You must not risk your safety, Mr Phillips. I will

not forget that you offered. And no doubt she will come around before you get halfway there.'

Speaking those words, he only half believed them. Felicia looked very pale. She lay utterly still and limp.

'Any of us would go, my lord. All of us are so very fond of Lady Scarsfeld.'

Three hours later Felicia was still limp and pale. Isaiah sat beside the bed watching her breathe, looking for any sort of expression to cross her face. A smile, a frown—even a grimace would do.

She was no longer cold. He was grateful to the staff for quickly heating bricks and tucking them into her bed. Within a quarter of an hour her hand had warmed in his.

He stroked her cheek. His fingers were colder than her skin. No doubt his face was paler than hers was, too.

Once again he stared loss in its ugly face.

Felicia might wake up and smile at him, but she might not. He could only guess how much damage the blow to her head had caused.

'Felicia?' he whispered close to her ear. Nothing. No tug of a lip or twitch of an eye.

'Felicia!' This time he shouted. Still, there she lay, as still as the branch that struck her.

'My Felicia…' His voice cracked on her name this time.

Whatever came, he would never regret the cost of loving her. Never again would he shutter his heart as he had done as a child.

He lay his head on the mattress beside her shoulder wanting to weep, needing that release.

Not that he would indulge in it. Doing so would toss him back to the past, to that bitter night when he had been inconsolable.

The past few hours hit him hard, trying their best to drag him back to the nightmare.

No matter what happened, he was not going back to the boy he had been, nor to the bitter man who had grown from the boy's sorrow.

He was changed for ever.

Besides, Felicia was not gone. Here she was where he could touch her and talk to her.

Directly behind him a sob erupted.

Straightening up from the bed, he gazed into Abigail's red, tearful eyes.

'Would you like to wait with me for her to wake?' He patted the cushion of the chair beside his.

She shook her head, bit her bottom lip. 'This is all my fault. If I hadn't gone to hide, it would not have happened.'

'No, sweetheart, this is not your fault at all.' He reached for her, but she backed away.

'If I hadn't lied and said I was going to join the circus, she would not have gone outside looking for me.'

'You could not have known she would.'

'Yes, I could.' She sniffled hard, wiping her sleeve across her nose.

'You are blaming yourself needlessly.'

'But I almost did go outside... I opened the door, but it was so cold I thought better of it. She must have noticed melted snow on the floor.'

'Felicia will not blame you for what happened.'

'But I don't even like the circus!'

'If your sister can hear you, there is a good chance she is laughing.'

'I'm sure that is not true.'

'Sit here with me, Abigail. Talk to Felicia while we wait for her to wake up.'

Sitting with a thump, she crossed her arms over her middle.

'I am too ashamed to speak to her.'

'Have you ever known her to be angry or hold a grudge?'

'Well, no. But I haven't known her all that long.'

'But you know her well enough.'

Abigail shrugged, clasping her hands tightly together on her lap.

'I present myself as proof of her forgiving heart,' he pointed out.

'Yes, you were rather a curmudgeon and yet here she is.'

'Tell her what is in your heart.'

'I'm sorry, Sister,' she murmured, her voice quavering. 'I never would have done any of it if I'd known you were going to go looking for me outside. Everyone was upset by what I did and they didn't even leave the house. Well, Mr Phillips did. And so did Lord Penfield. Isn't it odd how, of everyone, they frowned at me the least? They were so happy to find you, in their joy they quite overlooked what I had done. I suppose they will remember soon enough, though.'

'I'm sure she knows you regret it.'

'When you awaken you may reprimand me as much as you like. I will stand and take what I deserve.'

'You will not get what you deserve, not from Felicia. Neither did I.'

In order to comfort his sister he was encouraging her to believe Felicia could hear everything being spoken. Could she really, though? He had no idea.

'You should sing to her, Isaiah.' She shot him a blurry-eyed glance. 'If she can really hear you, she will appreciate it.'

A song might make these unbearable moments of waiting better for everyone.

Yes! Much in the way a bad memory could be banished by a good one? A moment and a memory were not so different. One simply happened before the other.

His bride had healed him in this way, perhaps he could…

'I need your help!' He stood so suddenly his chair tipped.

Abigail caught it, then set it upright. 'You wouldn't if you rose more carefully.'

'You have a smart mouth, miss. Never lose it.' He ruffled her hair, relieved to see the beginnings of a smile on her face. 'We are going to move the Christmas tree up here.'

'Oh, that will be grand! But why?'

'You know how partial Felicia is to it.'

Isaiah took long, quick steps towards the door. Abigail had to run to keep pace.

'She is devoted to it…luckily for me.'

'What do you mean?'

'I think you know, but I can be as forgiving as my sister is.'

'I'm grateful to hear it, for whatever crime I have

committed.' She could not know he had taken down her tree and Felicia had restored it. Could she?

'Do you expect her to revive for the joy over having the tree near her bed?'

'I hope it, only. But run and see who is available to help.'

He did not expect this to work, but he prayed most fervently that it would.

The darkness was comfortable. There was no cold, no pain, nothing at all unpleasant…just floating in a vast, soft nothing.

Oddly enough, there was also singing. It was all so very nice down here in the depths, listening to 'Jingle Bells,' 'What Child is This?' and 'O Come, O Come, Emmanuel.'

The last carol was the nicest. The singer's voice so full of emotion it nearly faltered over the words.

"'O come, O come, Emmanuel, to free your captive—'"

Oh, was that a sob? But why? It was so beautifully done. Surely the singer could have no regrets in his performance.

Even if he did, it was not her concern. All she needed to do was sink a bit deeper into darkness and concern for the singer's trouble slipped away.

Wasn't it strange that the darkness smelled like a Christmas tree? How very lovely.

"'On the first day of Christmas my true love sent to me…'"

Something jolted the dark. Her head began to ache. She tried to swim back down, but that something was drawing her, up and up.

"'A partridge in a pear tree...'"

That meant something to her! Whatever it was that jarred the peace beckoned her to float towards it. It seemed she ought to, but everything was so snug where she was.

The song went on. She heard 'five gold *r-i-i-ings*'!

Her body began to feel like—something. Not real, but no longer a vapour mingled in mist. No, she felt like a jellyfish being rolled upon the beach by a wave.

Five gold rings? Wait, she wore a ring on her finger. A wedding ring!

'Felicia!' Isaiah! That voice, so dear to her, sounded harsh with desperation. 'Come to me...follow my voice.'

It was easier where she was, in the nothingness. Yet she must try because she loved him.

Oh, but it was difficult, as if she were swimming in one of those dreams where one's movements were restrained by something unseen and threatening.

If she focused on his voice, calling to her...pleading with her...it was easier. She would do anything to prevent him from grieving because of her.

And then, there he was. Darkness receded, giving way to the greater power of light. His face looked fuzzy at first, but second by second it came into focus.

'Welcome home,' he whispered, his voice somewhere between a sob and rejoicing. 'You had us worried.'

She tried to ease up to her elbows, but everything went dizzy and she lay back.

'Why are you weeping, Isaiah?'

Oh...no! Something had happened to her and as a result of it she had she failed to find Abigail!

What had happened? One moment she had been calling for her sister and the next she was here.

'Abigail?' Why did her voice sound so weak? Surely only a few moments had passed.

'Aside from feeling wretched with guilt, she is well.'

'She is safe, then?' Felicia would have sagged in relief had she been able. As it was, she was pressed heavily against the mattress by her own weight. 'Where is she?'

'In bed.'

'At this time of day?'

'It is two in the morning.'

'Surely not!'

'You were unconscious for a long time.' He bent to kiss her cheek, then slid his mouth to gently kiss her lips.

'I do not remember any of it. What happened?'

'When you went to search for Abigail you were hit by a falling branch.'

'How did you find me?' He could not have known she'd run outside.

'You left the door cracked open so Lord Penfield and I went searching. But how I found you? I suspect it was by the grace of God.'

'Really?' She was beginning to think something along the same lines, but for a slightly different reason.

'I had no notion where to look. It was all blowing snow. Everything, even bushes, was invisible. Then a branch broke and I wondered if you might have been struck by one. I ran over and saw a strand of your hair peeking out of the snow.' She watched a shiver race over his shoulders. Reaching up, she wanted to smooth it away, but her hand fell back limp on the mattress.

It was hard to believe she had become this weak so quickly. That must be why it had been so difficult to come back, why the dark had been so deceptively peaceful.

What he must have been going through in those moments, probably recalling how he searched in vain for his mother, believing she had perished because he could not find her.

Knowing him as she did, she thought he would have been reliving that horror all over again, fearing he had lost another woman he loved.

She felt wretched that it had been her actions, no matter how well intentioned, which must have shot him to the nightmare of his past.

Horrible, wretched, yet perhaps, in the end, what had happened might be for his healing.

'I would like to sit.' She reached her arms up to him.

'Are you sure?'

'I've been lying far too long, have I not?'

He nodded, eased on to the bed, then positioned her so that she lay against his chest. His bent knees supported her on either side.

'This is so nice.' Carefully so that her head would not hurt, she shifted her gaze to the fireplace.

What? 'Isaiah, what have you done?'

'Brought the Christmas tree to you.'

'I don't believe it! Truly, you did this?'

'I had help with the moving, but the decorating? I did do that myself, took a long time at it, too.'

'I cannot even start to say how happy this makes me. I hope it was not too painful a thing to do.'

She felt the rise and fall of his breathing against her back. Oh, but she did cherish his strength and warmth. If only this moment could go on for ever.

But life was meant to be lived with all its joys and challenges. What a blessing it was that the two of them faced them together.

'It was, at first. But the strangest thing happened. Each time I hung one of them on a branch, memories came to me, good ones of me and my mother.' He nuzzled her neck gently, breathing in deeply where her pulse thrummed. 'I must confess something to you, Felicia.'

'Is it something delicious—perhaps even wicked?'

'Shocking more like it.'

'Truly?' She turned to look at him too quickly. Her vision went fuzzy, pain shot an arrow through her skull.

Isaiah lightly kissed her temple, erasing her wince.

'I confess it, I am glad you and Abigail brought home the Christmas tree. Don't let it get about, but I have grown very fond of the thing.'

'Now you are teasing me.'

'I would not. Not about a subject as serious as Christmas decor.'

'Decor? Pine cones and garlands are decor! A tree is more than that—somehow it feels as though the magic of Christmas is alive in its branches.'

'I'm the last person who would have thought it, but once again, you are right.'

'About Christmas, at least. And there is one other thing.'

'Only one?'

'It has to do with what you said about finding me by the grace of God. I wonder if what happened didn't only have to do with finding me, but with making some sort of peace with your past.'

'I did wonder that. I struggled with it—the feeling that somehow time had slipped backwards. If I had not found you, would I have gone back to being who I used to be?'

'You mustn't do that. No matter what happens to us over the years, you must promise me you will not.'

'The thing is, I didn't. When I feared the worst it was loving you that kept me from it.'

And she could say the same of his love. 'Do you know, Isaiah, when I was unconscious, I heard you singing—at first I wanted to stay where I was, but then I heard your love coming through it and I remembered us.'

'As long as we do that, we can face all the arrows coming at us, don't you think?'

'I do. Even the well-intentioned ones flung by the Penfields.'

'Especially those,' he said, then snugged his arms tighter about her. She grasped his hand where it rested close to her heart. 'I imagine I should spread the word that you have returned to us.'

'I imagine so.'

He made no move to do it.

'Let me hold you a while longer,' he murmured into her ear. 'When you are ready I will get us some tea.'

'Some of our best times have involved tea.'

'Some of them, but lately…' his voice grew low and husky, tickling the hair near her ear '…our tea would grow cold before we gave it a thought.'

And so they sat in silence, feeling each other breathe, wrapped up in the relief of being together.

She must have started to doze because she was startled awake by a soft knock on the door.

Mrs Muldoon came inside carrying, of all things, a tea tray.

'Oh! My lady, you have returned to us. I knew it was the right thing to bring two cups.'

Isaiah's muscles shifted as if he would get up to take the tray.

'Ach, no! Stay where you are, my lord.'

Cook shuffled about, pulling over a small table and setting the tea and cups on it. There were also pastries which made Felicia feel half-queasy to look at.

'I shall spread the good news.' Even as late as it was and the lady ought to have been abed, she smiled brightly at them.

'There is no need to wake anyone.'

'Wake them?' Mrs Muldoon laughed quietly. 'Everyone is gathered in the parlour, waiting for news.'

'Surely not!' Felicia tried to exclaim, but only croaked.

'And where else would they be, my lady? But I will tell them and they will take to their beds soon enough.'

With that she bustled out of the chamber.

'Do you know,' she said. 'I feel that I am completely at home.'

'No matter where we are, wherever we go, this place

right here…' He hugged her tighter to him, she thought, in order to make sure she knew where here was. 'You will always be at home.'

Chapter Fourteen

In the morning, the first person to come hesitantly into Felicia's chamber was Abigail.

Her face looked far too sombre. She was a child, one who ought to be smiling. She clutched Eloise tight to her chest. It was a wonder the cat did not struggle to get out of her arms.

There was nothing Felicia could do about her sadness if the reason for it had to do with what she had discovered about the Penfields wanting to take her with them.

If, on the other hand, it had to do with feeling guilty for Felicia venturing out in the storm in search of her, she could do quite a bit about that.

'Sit here beside me.'

Felicia patted her mattress. Abigail set the cat on Felicia's lap and then climbed up on the tall bed.

'Can you tell me why you look so sad?'

'I nearly killed you. If my brother had not found you when he did, I would be a murderer.'

'Silly little bird.' She ruffled Abigail's hair. 'You were the one clever enough to remain indoors, not me.'

'But you thought I was in danger, it was why you went out.'

'You must understand, it was my choice and I would do it again.'

'The need will not arise. I promise it will not.'

'I should have known you had sense enough not to. This was more my fault than yours. And in the end, no harm was done.'

'But there was! Tomorrow is Christmas and you are stuck in bed.'

'And the tree is stuck in my room.' She would need to get Isaiah to move it back downstairs so that everyone could enjoy it. Father Christmas could hardly deliver his gifts to Felicia's chamber, after all. 'Besides, I am perfectly well. It's only that your brother will not allow me to get out of bed yet.'

'Truly? You are feeling recovered?'

'Completely.' Nearly that, at any rate.

'I will be downstairs in the morning to see what Father Christmas has brought you.'

'If I have your forgiveness, nothing he brings will be as good as that.'

'I hold no ill feelings towards you, little Sister. I love you too much for that.'

'Isaiah told me you would not, since you didn't hold a grudge against him either and we both know he deserved it.'

'For any particular crime?'

'For taking down our Christmas tree and then making you put it back and sleep under it to keep him from doing it again.'

It only hurt Felicia's head a little to laugh, which

was a relief. With Christmas so near she was ready for merriment. Troubling matters could be put away for a day. She had every intention of having a joyful time with those she cared for. Among whom were Lord and Lady Penfield.

They could only feel wretched over what happened. All they wanted was a family and, as far as Felicia could tell, they would be devoted parents.

But sometimes good intentions went awry. Her going out into the storm was a perfect example. Her thought had been to save, but had her husband not found her it would have brought heartache upon them all.

'Do you like Eloise?' Abigail asked, her expression brightening somewhat.

'Indeed I do, she is a wonderful cat.'

'Good, then. I will leave her here with you.' She placed Eloise in her lap, then petted her slowly from nose to tail. 'To keep you company for the afternoon. You can become great friends with her.'

With that, Abigail got off the bed and hurried towards the door.

Before closing it behind her, she turned to say, 'I'm very grateful to have a sister, no matter what else happens.'

'And I am grateful to have your company, Miss Eloise. I could be up and about were not someone so much stronger than I am forbidding it.'

It was Christmas morning!

Isaiah would have sprung from the bed had not Felicia been sleeping so peacefully beside him.

But it was Christmas and he had not felt the thrill of rising to greet it in far too many years.

He bounced on the mattress to judge how deeply Felicia was asleep.

One bleary-looking green eye blinked open.

He bent over her to peer into that one eye. 'It's morning!'

'Good morning.' She rolled over on her side, snuggling into the pillow.

'Good Christmas morning!' He bounced more forcefully this time. 'It's nearly daylight.'

This time she opened both eyes, a smile shining in them. 'Is it light already? How could you let me oversleep?'

She tried to bolt out of bed. He caught her balance before she toppled.

'Hand me my robe and slippers.' She wagged her finger impatiently at the chairs where they lay in a heap on the cushion. 'We must get down before Abigail does! I can't wait to watch her come down the stairs and see all that Father Christmas has brought. It was such a beautiful sight I could hardly sleep with all the excitement.'

He nearly laughed because she had given an excellent impression of a deep night's sleep.

Going down the steps, he could tell she was much stronger than she had been last night. For all that it was encouraging, he had no intention of letting go of her until they stepped into the parlour.

As it turned out, they were not the first to come down.

Lord Penfield and Lady Penfield stood beside the window, the merrily snapping Yule log casting a happy glow over everything. Judging by the grins on their faces, the Penfields were as excited as the Scarsfelds were.

It sounded nice in his mind. The Scarsfelds—Isaiah and Felicia Scarsfeld. Lord and Lady Scarsfeld.

He wondered what people would think if he held a party here at Scarsfeld. It would be appropriate to properly introduce his wife—appropriate and a great joy.

His neighbours were no doubt wondering why he had wed so quickly. As soon as they met Felicia they would understand—applaud him, even, for his wise choice in a bride.

Yet he had had been very lucky, very blessed.

'I hope you don't mind us rising so early,' Lady Penfield said, her expression bright and sparkling. 'It is a thrill to be able to spend Christmas with a child. To share the excitement of Father Christmas's visit. I'll admit we were both restless with excitement all night long.'

Isaiah and his supposed foes had that in common. Of course, it was difficult to think of them in that light any longer. Not with all they had been through and with their shared affection for Abigail.

Apparently Mrs Muldoon was awake as well for the Penfields each held a cup of what smelled like hot chocolate.

'I think the sun will be shining today,' Lord Penfield commented. 'The sky is bright and starry.'

'Yes.' Lady Penfield sighed. 'As much as we have so truly enjoyed staying with you, if the weather permits we must be going home tomorrow.'

Abigail's footsteps on the stairs prevented him from

asking if it was still their intention to take his sister with them.

Maybe he should continue to fight, but not this morning.

Peace on earth, good will towards men, was what the day was about. For the first time in what seemed for ever, he felt the sentiment fill him up.

Abigail bounded into the parlour, her injury seeming to be healed or forgotten.

'He came!'

'But of course he did.' Lady Penfield stood, clapped her hands then took a place beside Abigail while she danced and spun in front of her pile of gifts. 'Father Christmas always comes.'

'I thought I might get a lump of coal.'

'You see…' Felicia walked slowly over towards the pair '…even Santa believes you did not misbehave.'

Then something happened that he would have believed impossible on the day he read Lord Penfield's letter.

Abigail wriggled into the space between her sister and her aunt, wrapping one arm around each of them. The ladies, in turn, hugged each other's shoulders.

Of all the gifts happily waiting under the tree, the one he was looking at would outshine them all.

Lord Penfield glanced at him, cleared his throat, but made no move to engage Isaiah in a hug.

As for the gifts wrapped under the tree, there were more of them than had been there when he and Felicia had gone up for the night. The Penfields must have come prepared to spread cheer.

Again, not at all what he had expected them to spread.

Abigail dipped out from the hug, snatched a present and waggled it at them.

'Now?'

'Now.' Isaiah nodded, feeling a grin reach all the way to his toes.

Gift opening began sedately enough, but soon dissolved into beautiful chaos.

To his surprise, Lady Penfield presented gifts to him and to Felicia.

Laughter, hugs, and good wishes were what this day was all about.

More than that, it was what family was all about.

This, what was happening in his parlour right now, was what he had been missing all his life. Yet when it had first arrived he had distrusted it, had judged his sister's family to be a threat.

Of course, he had not been the only one. In the beginning he and Lord Penfield had gone at each other as adversaries. Yet here they were, discovering that friendship was better than ill will. If only a decision did not stretch painfully between them, their joy in each other's company would be complete.

He hoped that when tomorrow came, the spirit of December the twenty-fifth would slip into December the twenty-sixth.

But tomorrow was coming. In the morning the Penfields would be going home and things would be strained.

'This is so beautiful, Abigail!' he heard Felicia exclaim. 'Thank you so much.'

'It is from Eloise. The feathers are not from birds that she caught.'

'That is a great relief.'

To his way of thinking, Felicia's laugh was the first of the carols they would sing.

This was a day of days and he would not allow himself to think beyond it.

Felicia had to admit that the morning after Christmas was strained. Although Abigail sat at the table with them, it was as if she was not there.

Who would expect anything different, given what she must be going through?

Worry etched lines on her husband's face. He picked up a piece of toast, set it down, then tried to sip his tea. The wonder was that he did not choke on it.

Of all the people in this house, he alone fully understood what it was like to be ripped from home.

'It was such a lovely Christmas,' Felicia said because anything was better than this silence. 'What was your favourite gift, Abigail?'

'There were many wonderful gifts.' She looked at her plate while she spoke. 'Spending time with my aunt and uncle—that was my favourite.'

'It was,' Isaiah said, his fingers turning white gripping his spoon, 'a very great pleasure to have them visit.'

But there was one thing puzzling her. The Penfields were going home to London this morning. Were they taking this child with them or were they not?

They ought to have said, one way or another. Abigail was not the only one who would suffer the heartache of the coming decision. There were four adults in the house—two of them would end up heartbroken.

Eloise strode into the room, leaping from the floor to Abigail's lap. Abigail picked her up, rubbing her face against the cat's cheek. Then, with a great sigh, she set her pet on the floor. 'Shoo, go away!'

Shoo...go away? Felicia had never heard her sister say such a thing to her cat. Two days ago she had fed Eloise a quarter of a piece of ham, then cooed to her while carrying her from the dining room.

All of a sudden she stood up, chased after the cat. Pausing in the doorway, she looked back at them. 'I love you both very much.'

The pair she had mentioned stared silently at the kick of her petticoat as she fled into the hallway.

Isaiah placed his hand on the table, palm up, wordlessly asking for comfort.

At least this, their marriage and their love, came of this turmoil. It was the silver lining they must cling to.

So she did cling to his offered hand, to give support as much as to get it.

'Whatever happens this morning, I must say nothing that will add to my sister's pain. If I have to smile and pretend I am happy for her great opportunity to live in London, it is what I will do.'

'If you smile, she will know you do not mean it. Better that you look at the toes of your boots when you lie.'

'Or at you. I will look at you and you will pass the smile to Abigail.'

'Should we refuse to let them have her? We could take them to court.'

'It would be a long and painful thing to do. Whatever good will has grown between us and them would be destroyed. The lawyers would see to that.'

'But it might take a very long to be resolved. She would stay with us for that long,' she pointed out.

'I hear what you are saying, Felicia, and I think you do not mean it, not in your heart. Those are words meant for my comfort.' He squeezed her hand hard, but she did not tell him it hurt a bit. 'We will appear happy for her, no matter what occurs.'

'And we will travel to London as often as we are able,' she said.

'I used to hate London, but I suppose if my sister is there I will tolerate it.'

'London can be lovely, you know. You will see it for yourself when we visit my family.' She touched his frown, trying to smooth it away. 'And perhaps they do not intend to take her at all. Perhaps it is why they have not informed us of it.'

'Maybe you are right. As long as I have you, I can bear whatever happens.'

And so she gave him a kiss, hoping he understood it was the promise of a lifetime.

Three hours later, Mr Phillips entered Isaiah's office to inform him that the carriage had been brought round and the Penfields were in the hall, waiting to bid their farewells.

Dreading this moment, he had hidden from it by burying his attention in the ledgers. With the butler standing in the doorway he could hardly ignore it any longer.

'Do you know where my sister is, Mr Phillips?'

'I believe she is in her chamber with Miss Shirls.'

The Penfields were packed, ready to depart and waiting in the hall. Abigail was not with them.

Hope surged in his heart, pumping in his blood to his feet and back.

Had they intended to take her they would have said so and she would not be in her room! No, Abigail would be waiting with her aunt and uncle to go out to the coach.

'Where is my wife?' he asked on half a run across the office.

He could be wrong about this. But, no, he thought he was not!

'In the hall, my lord, saying farewell to your guests.'

By the time he burst into the hall his heart was beating hard, nearly slamming against his ribs.

Lady Penfield smiled when she saw him. She hurried across the carpet and took his hands in hers.

'Getting to know you has been a great joy,' she said and he knew she meant it. The lady had never been anything but sincere.

The only luggage being carried to the coach was that which they had brought in with them when they arrived.

Lord Penfield stepped forward and extended his hand.

Isaiah did not take it, but instead wrapped the man in a brief hug, then pounded his back.

'I meant to tell you, something, Henry.' He cleared his throat to ease what he had to say. Oddly, he realised this was going to be easier than he would have expected. 'Thank you for trying to help my mother—for trying to be the son she left behind.'

'It would not have worked. You were her flesh and blood. That is much too strong a bond to try to replace. In truth, I'm not sure it is even possible.'

From the corner of his eye he saw Felicia and Lady Penfield hugging and probably shedding a tear or two.

Isaiah felt a lump in his throat to be saying goodbye to the Penfields, but weeping—well—he and Lord Penfield would leave that to be expressed by their wives.

'We will visit you in London,' he said. Funny how he truly wanted to. 'Now that Abigail has got to know her family—that we have got to know you—we will miss you.'

'Given the reason we came here, I would not have expected it.'

He slipped his arm over Lord Penfield's shoulder in a companionable way and lowered his voice. 'Do you know, I would never be a married man had you not come? You were right when you accused me of making a convenient marriage and disguising it as a love match. But it is not that now and I have you to thank for it.'

Lord Penfield laughed out loud, slamming his open palm on Isaiah's back. 'I'm no fool, Isaiah. The fact is clear to see. I fully expect to see you carrying a babe in your arms when next we meet.'

How could he respond to that? He could not. Not when it was what the Penfields wanted with their whole hearts.

They might have had what they longed for in his sister, but had chosen not to break up the family she already had.

It would be his nightly prayer that the Penfields would have the family they wanted so desperately.

'Where is our niece?' Lady Penfield asked. 'We cannot leave without saying goodbye to her.'

'Here I am,' came Abigail's voice, sounding younger and more subdued than he had ever heard. 'You need not say goodbye, Aunt. I have decided to come and live with you.'

He must have gasped out loud, because she looked down at him, blinking furiously.

'I'm sorry, Isaiah!' While she stood ringing her hands, Miss Shirls came on to the landing, dressed for travel and carrying three valises, one in each hand and one tucked under her arm. 'It is a wonderful opportunity and—and I think, well, it is what I am called to do in order to make amends for nearly killing Felicia.'

Lady Penfield clasped her hand over her mouth, turning her startled gaze to her husband.

'A penance, do you mean, my dear?' Lord Penfield asked.

'Yes, but I have grown fond of you, Uncle, and my aunt, too. So I'm not quite throwing myself on the sacrificial fire.'

'But ought you to let your poor cat suffer?' Lady Penfield asked. 'She will miss you, you know.'

Abigail seemed to have nothing to say to that. But Isaiah knew that in her heart she was making a great sacrifice for what, in her very young heart, she considered her duty.

Felicia came to him, insinuating herself under his arm. Had his body begun to sag the same as his heart had?

Here was Lord Penfield and Lady Penfield's dream handed to them on a platter, so to speak. All that needed doing was for one of them to raise an arm in welcome and Abigail would come down the steps and go with them into the coach.

Even without that she did come down.

Going to Felicia first, she gazed up at her. 'I am grateful to have a sister. Eloise has asked if you will love her in my place.'

'Of course I will, but—'

Lord Penfield and Lady Penfield stared at each other in some silent communication that long-married couples were so adept at.

Next thing he knew, Abigail threw her small arms around him, hugging tightly.

She began to weep. She had made what she considered to be a brave decision, but she was only eight years old and could not hide the emotions that came along with her choice.

'I love you, Isaiah…' She wiped her nose on his sleeve. 'I will never…but you will come to visit…and—'

Lady Penfield touched Abigail's small, trembling shoulder, turning her away from him.

Cupping Abigail's face in her plump hands, hands that Isaiah noticed shook a bit, she bent and kissed her forehead.

'You really are the bravest girl, Abigail. I am proud to call you my niece. But you see, your uncle and I, well, we would be so grateful if you were to come and visit. But…'

Lady Penfield cast a look at her husband, her eyes blinking back tears.

'The thing is,' Lord Penfield continued when his wife

had difficulty finding the words, 'your aunt and I feel you are happy where you are.'

'I will learn to be happy with you.'

'But what your uncle and I were thinking is that it is not fair for one sweet girl to have two families to live with and be adored by them both, when there is a child out in the world who has no family to love them.'

'We hoped you would not mind,' Lord Penfield said, his voice going low and strained, 'sharing us with a less fortunate child.'

'You mean I needn't go—that is—it would be more a penance to stay here and make up for my wrongdoing?'

'Oh, indeed,' he answered. 'Giving another child a chance at a family would more than make up for that.'

Abigail hugged her uncle tight. 'I will miss you every day, Uncle Henry!'

'As I will miss you, child.'

Isaiah knew how deeply he meant those words because Lord Penfield looked steadily the ceiling while he spoke.

'Next Christmas you shall visit London!' Lady Penfield exclaimed. 'We shall have the best and brightest time. But come now, Henry, let us be on our way before we wear out our welcome.'

'You could never do that, my dear friend,' Felicia said, holding Lady Penfield by both hands and kissing her cheek.

Moments later the Penfields were gone.

The house seemed very quiet—too quiet.

Had there really been a time when he preferred it this way?

What a fool he had been, a wounded one, but a fool

just the same. Now that Felicia had let his heart out of its dreary iron safe, he was never looking back at it.

In his mind, he picked it up and tossed it on to a fire so hot it melted, never to be made into anything ever again—except perhaps for a dozen keys to a dozen houses where a dozen happy families lived.

And for all that his wife and his sister stared mournfully at the closed front door, they were a happy family.

Joyful, blessed and in need of—

'As I recall it, the two of you owe me a rematch of our snowball fight. The sun is shining and I say you must pay up.'

'You might be sorry.' Felicia turned to him, the smile he loved playing happily on her lips.

'I'll run upstairs and get Eloise! She will not want to miss your defeat!'

Abigail dashed up the stairs laughing, twirling about on every other step and acting every bit the eight-year-old girl she was.

'Do you know what day this is, Felicia?' He held his arms wide and she stepped into them.

'December the twenty-sixth.' She snuggled into him with a wiggle.

'Yes, and yet it still feels like Christmas. Why is that, do you think?'

'I do not think, Isaiah. I know. The love that came down at Christmas was not for one day only. Even after the carols have been sung, the gifts opened and the feasts eaten, it carries on to fill us with the strength we need to face whatever comes the rest of the year.'

'Well then, I am armed with love and ready to face whatever it is.'

'For all the good it will do you in our snowball fight!' Abigail cried while racing past them towards the conservatory, the cat dangling rag-like from the crook of her elbow.

'Just hold that love until tonight, Husband, we shall see what kind of strength you need.'

Felicia kissed him lightly, then tugged on his hand to urging him towards the battle.

London—December 20, 1890

It did not appear that it was going to snow while Felicia snipped branches. Given that the clouds dotting the sky were no more than wispy puffs, it was not likely to drizzle either. Yet she smiled while cutting greenery in the Penfield garden.

'If the weather was any more pleasant, I would outright weep for joy.' Lady Penfield cut a branch of spruce and set it in the basket looped over her arm.

'I will confess, my friend—or whatever relation we might be, I have not been quite able to pinpoint what it is called—that this is a lovely day.'

'It is great fun to see ladies walking and showing off their fine gowns,' Abigail pointed out while reaching for a clump of berries to snip.

'Oh, and the bonnets! Are they not the most delicious things you have ever seen?' Lady Penfield asked.

Clearly, Felicia's young sister was taken with London fashion, sighing and pointing to every pretty frill they spotted parading past the garden gate.

'You will be parading with them in only nine more

years, my girl. I can hardly wait to present you to society.'

Nine years did not seem nearly long enough to Felicia. Time went by too quickly. She could scarcely believe she and Isaiah had just celebrated their first anniversary.

'Tell me, Felicia, how was your visit with your family?'

'Wonderful. For all that we spent a lovely week with them, we are glad to be spending Christmas with you.'

'We are so happy you came. Truly, we have missed you every day since we left Scarsfeld.'

'Eloise wandered about searching for you for a week,' Abigail said. 'I would have brought her, but Isaiah thought it better not to. I see he was right about it. I can hardly believe so many people live in one place.'

'It is not as lovely here as where you live, of course, but there are many things to do. When you are of age I shall enjoy showing you each and every one of them.'

'I think I will find a kind and handsome nobleman to wed among so many people.'

'You might, my dear, but you must be open to finding such a man anywhere.' She smiled at Felicia. 'Your family must be relieved to see with their own eyes how successful your marriage is. Some arrangements between strangers go all wrong.'

'But sometimes they go very, very right.'

'I would imagine your sister, Ginny, was relieved that you and Isaiah have made a success of things.'

'Greatly relieved. I have only just discovered she took to her room for a week, overcome with remorse that she did not step in to fulfil our mother's wish.' It had taken a very private talk with her sister to convince her that she was as happily married as she appeared to be.

'And your other sister is wed, I understand?'

'Yes, for six months now. Peter has yet to settle down.'

A step on the terrace drew their attention.

'My lady, the children are ready to be put down for their naps.' The nursemaid crossed the garden, a child in each of her arms.

'Well, my darlings, come to Mother, then.' Lady Penfield's smile was all happiness as she set down her basket and reached for her daughters, one about a year old and the other about three.

They were thought to be sisters at the orphanage run by Lady Fencroft. The Countess had found them together on a poor, mean street in town, the older one holding the younger in her skinny little arms.

Knowing that Lord and Lady Penfield were looking for a child to adopt, she brought them straight away to Penfield, where they remained.

'There is not a day that I do not thank the good lady who brought them here. Few people care any longer that she was an American heiress who snatched up an eligible earl. No one can match her in good works for London's poor children.' Giving each small girl a kiss, she carried them back towards the house. 'I will see you at tea, Felicia,' she called over her shoulder.

'So will I.' Abigail snatched up her aunt's basket and hurried after her and the children.

Abigail loved babies. Indeed, she had not mentioned

missing Eloise since she first set eyes upon the little girls this morning.

Felicia continued to cut greenery while listening to the sounds she had not heard in a long time. The music of life in London was vastly different than the less hectic music of life at Scarsfeld.

Truthfully, she enjoyed them both, but in the end she would be happy to return home where the creak of carriage wheels beyond the gate and the sound of a dozen voices all coming to her as one indiscernible murmur would be replaced with the peaceful sough of wind tickling treetops.

As if thinking of tickling had summoned it, a rush of air shivered her neck.

A very special rush of air, one that she knew intimately.

'I challenge you to a duel with holly branches since there is not a snowball to be had,' her husband whispered in her ear. 'With our little sister involved with babies, it will be a more even match. One against one.'

'Here is your weapon, sir.' She handed him a short, prickly-leaved branch, then chose a longer one for herself.'

She took a pose, waving her weapon under his nose. 'Be ready to meet your doom, my—'

He struck before she was ready, the sly fellow. He tossed her weapon into a bush and his after it.

'I suppose I must pay a forfeit.' She touched his lips with her fingertips. It had been a year and still she did not tire of touching them. 'I imagine it will be something wicked that I will regret very soon.'

'Later tonight you will pay, for now I will take a kiss.'

He did, a very long and lingering one.

'Here,' she said, picking up the shears which Lady Penfield had left behind. 'You may be useful between now and then. Now that you no longer dislike Christmas decorations, this will be fun.'

'I no longer dislike Christmas trees. Having ribbons and lace tangled up in my fingers is quite another matter.'

'For now we will snip and talk.'

He took the basket from her arm and slung it over his much stronger one.

The shears went click, click, click, nearly making a melody.

'If we time the cutting just so, I think we can play "Jingle Bells."'

'Only someone named Felicia Merry would think of such a thing.'

'Let us try, then we will explore your name meaning. We never did fully discover why it fits.'

While they clicked the blades in tune, Isaiah sang along. Somehow he made the piece sound very nice. She would have joined in the singing, but she thought she ought not to.

'God is salvation and has judged mercifully,' he quit singing to say. 'It is not a contradiction. It suits my life rather well.'

Felicia set down her shears, then traced the line of his jaw where he was in need of a shave. She never tired of touching him there, either. There was not an inch of the man she grew weary of touching.

He set down the basket and looked up an inch to hold her gaze.

'God did judge me mercifully and with a bit of humour. Did he not?'

'I think you will need to explain it to me.'

'Well…' He twirled a slipped lock of hair in his finger. There were areas of her body he never seemed to tire of touching as well, her hair being one of them. 'He found a crusty grump of a fellow and gave him a woman named Felicia Merry.'

'And he gave me a man with the most beautiful singing voice. A man I can never hope to sing to and have it come out anything but a screech.'

'No, my dear wife, you sing to me every single day. Your heart sings me a carol which makes it Christmas every day and nothing is more beautiful to my ears.'

'Oh, well…then. Shall I carry on with our song?'

'Yes, let us make Christmas a lifelong affair.'

Then he kissed her—and it was.

* * * * *